THE TIGERS OF TABOO VALLEY

Ranjit Lal has written books for both adults and children. Some of his books include *The Crow Chronicles*, *The Life and Times of Altu-Faltu*, *Bossman and the Kala Shaitan*, *Birds from My Window*. He has been a winner of the Crossword Best Children's Book Award for *Faces in the Water*.

Ranjit Lal

RED TURTLE
RUPA

Published in Red Turtle by
Rupa Publications India Pvt. Ltd 2014
7/16, Ansari Road, Daryaganj
New Delhi 110002

Sales Centres:

Prayagraj Bengaluru Chennai
Hyderabad Jaipur Kathmandu
Kolkata Mumbai

Copyright © Ranjit Lal 2014

This is a work of fiction. Names, characters, places and incidents are either the product of the author's imagination or are used fictitiously and any resemblance to any actual person, living or dead, events or locales is entirely coincidental.

All rights reserved
No part of this publication may be reproduced, transmitted, or stored in a retrieval system, in any form or by any means, electronic, mechanical, photocopying, recording or otherwise, without the prior permission of the publisher.

P-ISBN: 978-81-291-3004-4
E-ISBN: 978-81-291-3249-9

Fourteenth impression 2023

20 19 18 17 16 15 14

The moral right of the author has been asserted.

Printed in India

This book is sold subject to the condition that it shall not, by way of trade or otherwise, be lent, resold, hired out, or otherwise circulated, without the publisher's prior consent, in any form of binding or cover other than that in which it is published.

For Juhi—this was long overdue

1

Rana Shaan-Bahadur, the most macho and royal of the Royal Bengal tigers of Sher-kila National Park, yawned and stretched as the first golden rays of the sun set his coat afire. His Personal Assistant and Press Secretary, Naradmunni the jackal, swept up dust with his tail and smiled ingratiatingly as he crawled towards him, head between paws.

'Huzoor, I bring glad tidings on this golden morn! The world-famous photographer from the *National Geographic*, the beautiful raven-haired Ayesha, has arrived at the Rest House. And even as we speak, she could be setting forth into the park to take pictures in the gilded light of this new dawn...'

Shaan-Bahadur's green eyes glittered. 'Eh? What the hell are you talking about?' Then understanding glimmered. 'Is that so? I'd better go down to the waterhole and make sure I'm looking good...' Actually, it was the first thing Shaan-Bahadur did every morning—look at his reflection and make sure that every whisker was perfectly groomed and positioned, and his coat glowed like the interior of Popacatapetl volcano.

'Huzoor, do forgive me, but you always look so noble. You are the most handsome tiger in the country, even in the morning when you awake, with bits of grass sticking out from your head and ears and your dragon's breath that can render a rhinoceros unconscious at twenty feet!' Naradmunni rolled his eyes and reeled as if he were about to faint.

'You talk too much!' Shaan-Bahadur growled and made his way down the rocky path. The waterhole was some distance away, surrounded by high elephant grass with only one winding path leading to and from it. Shaan-Bahadur had often crouched behind the grass, at a bend, waiting for prey and had scored many kills here. In the summer, when most of the other waterholes dried up, many animals had no choice but to come here to drink.

This morning however, well before sunrise, there had been visitors of a different, sinister kind. Two men in khaki shorts and shirts, carrying something which had terrible steel jaws. They had stopped on the path near one of the spots from where Shaan-Bahadur had launched many an ambush and then nodded to each other, keeping their torches well hooded. They were armed, and while one looked around nervously, the other began his work. It took him longer than he thought it would because the soil was rock hard and by the time he finished, the sun had turned the waters to gold.

Unknown to them, Ayesha the beautiful raven-haired photographer from the *National Geographic*, had also risen very early, coiled her tresses into a neat bun at the nape of her neck and had set out in a Gypsy towards the waterhole in the hope of photographing the animals and birds that came there to drink and bathe. Normally, of course, visitors were not allowed unescorted into the park, but Ayesha, a prize-winning photographer and wildlife film-maker, was from the *National Geographic* after all. She had beautiful silky hair and the most wonderful curling eyelashes (framing big black eyes) that anyone (and certainly the Field Director) had ever seen...

'Jaldi karo!' the second man now said. 'The sun's risen!'

'You just stand around farting, don't tell me to hurry up!' the first man snapped irritably. 'Come on now, it's done! Let's go! We'll check again at dusk.'

They packed up their digging equipment and started to walk back around the bend...

...And came face to face with Shaan-Bahadur!

'Yaaaa, mummy bachao!' they shouted and backed away, white in the face, too petrified to raise their guns.

'Grrrrrowwwrrr!' Shaan-Bahadur roared, equally startled. He roared again and then turned and fled, leaping through the grass as though the devil was behind him.

Phattack! went the trap as one of the men tripped backwards on top of it, its jaws snapping shut on his bottom.

'Owww! Pakad liya!' he howled, clutching his bum and trying to free it of those merciless jaws. The other man panicked and dived into the waterhole forgetting that tigers were good swimmers… and anyway now Magar and Machch, the crocodiles who owned it, were languidly swimming towards him.

'Breakfast is served, darling,' Magar murmured, grinning.

'You are too kind, my sweet!' Machch said, flipping his tail.

'Oh my God!' Ayesha, breathed as she squinted through her viewfinder, her finger firmly pressed on the camera's shutter button. She had parked her Gypsy at a vantage point and had seen (and photographed) everything. Well, almost everything: she'd got the face-to-face meeting between the men and the tiger and the poachers falling back, but (happily) not any shots of Shaan-Bahadur fleeing through the grass.

Within hours the photographs were everywhere, on the Internet, on YouTube, on Facebook, on every TV news channel. To say they had gone viral would be completely inadequate.

Before seven o'clock that morning, Rana Shaan-

Bahadur had become the world's most famous tiger—the only tiger to have caught poachers in their own trap. He was an international celebrity!

'Holy chital,' muttered Ugly Thug, the park's Beta-male (no prizes for guessing who the alpha male was), 'now his head is going to swell like a watermelon!' He shook his own massive head. His chances of becoming boss tiger had diminished considerably. As it is all the tigresses in the park, Raat-ki-Raani, Resham, Razia and Lolita, went weak at the knees and behaved in a disgracefully coy manner when Shaan-Bahadur walked past them.

Naradmunni, of course, was ecstatic. '*National Geographic*, BBC, CNN, NDTV, ABC, DEF, GHI…! Boss, you name the channel and you're on it!'

Shaan-Bahadur made the most of his celebrity status. He changed his Facebook profile photo every half hour. He posed statuesquely at sunrise and sunset when photographers get the best light, on the ramparts of the Sher-kila. He roared and snarled ferociously, he conducted mock charges, he tried very hard to be photographed while actually hunting, but the stupid chital didn't cooperate and ran away behind some high grass… He was magnificent.

Tigresses as a rule are not in the habit of gossiping (or kitty partying), but after Shaan-Bahadur's rise to stardom, they couldn't help messaging each other frantically by squirting on their 'walls' (tree trunks) and calling.

'I'm going to have his cubs,' Raat-ki-Rani announced proudly as the others growled jealously. It was true... Three or four months ago Naradmunni had smugly informed the others that Shaan-Bahadur and Raat-ki-Rani were an 'item'.

Well, their turn would come. Shaan-Bahadur was notoriously fickle and changed his mates frequently. Also, he wanted to father every single cub in the park. In the meanwhile, the other tigresses had to accept types like Thug and Taimur and Caligua.

'Sure, but last time he walked past me, he gave me *that look*!' Razia now messaged with a delicious shudder. 'You know what that means? Turned my knees to water, I can tell you.'

'And he pretended to drive me away from a kill I had made,' Lolita replied. 'I know the silly fellow was only flirting!'

'Did you run away?' Resham questioned bitingly.

'I was honoured that he ate at my table,' Lolita replied with great dignity. 'And he ate everything!'

'Sure, sure!' the others chorused, 'Of course he would!'

'I'm the one he's really after,' Razia squirted smugly. 'He ignores me, and that's the first sign that he's interested. One day he'll...'

'Keep on dreaming, darling.'

Soon, though, the outside world, in its usual fickle way, lost interest and drifted away. Not that it made any difference to Shaan-Bahadur; his head remained swollen as a pumpkin. He made sure that no tiger in the park ever forgot his deed. If any tiger or tigress did not show him the respect and deference he thought they should, they received a swift swipe to the head and a jet of urine up their noses, accompanied by a roar: 'Do you know who I am, you hyena-striped scumbag? Now grovel!'

There was however, one person who was still interested in him: Ayesha, the beautiful raven-haired photographer. She had often wondered what had happened to him that morning; she had been so busy photographing the poachers falling into their trap and jumping into the waterhole that she had not seen what had become of him. Had he, in the manner of the best heroes, done his brave deed and vanished like a phantom super tiger? Of course, very soon afterwards, he had been photographed scores of times, posing statuesquely on the fort, but was that because he was clever? By letting the paparazzi and visitors photograph him was he ensuring that they wouldn't bother him at other times, when he wanted his privacy?

She was determined to find out what he did in his 'private' time and photograph his private life.

2

Raat-ki-Rani leapt fluidly up the flat step-like rocks until she was nearly at the top of the rock-face. From here she got a panoramic view of Sher-kila National Park. Surrounded by rocky escarpments that tumbled into deep ravines, it had large patches of dense teak and sal forest that encircled grassy meadows where the chital and sambar grazed and wild boar piglets chased each other. She could see Magar and Machch's waterhole too, surrounded as it was by its elephant grass. It was a good place for a tiger; the dense forests were perfect for hiding in, from where you could watch the deer in the meadows. Invariably, they would drift closer to the forest's edge, and if you had anticipated where the herd would reach, and wriggled near that spot, you could launch your attack with a very good chance of making a kill. Then all you had to do was haul it into the shade of the trees away from prying eyes. There were streams and pools in the ravines, ideal for cooling off on a hot summer's day after you had eaten your fill and hidden your kill.

Of course, that selfish (if extremely handsome) lout, Shaan-Bahadur had claimed a huge area around the waterhole for himself, but the park was extensive and so far at least, there had been enough space for all the tigers inhabiting it. He did tolerate the occasional visit from pretty tigresses into his area.

She stared at the almost sheer rock-face looming up far behind her into the sky like a high prison wall: behind it she knew lay Taboo Valley, the forbidden forest; lush and lovely but now so accursed that no predator—not even Shaan-Bahadur dared venture there.

Raat-ki-Rani looked at the park spread below her, green and gold, thickly forested, studded with sapphire blue waterholes and small lakes. A white-backed vulture everyone called Diclo glided swiftly past her, glancing at her, the wind hissing through his pinions. He was followed by his wife Fenac, and instinctively the tigress growled. They were nothing but thieves, even if they did occasionally help indicate a kill, which you could then steal for yourself... She turned around and slipped into a crack in the rock-face. It opened into a snug, cozy cave, the perfect place for a nursery. Being a sensible and experienced tigress, she had earmarked three other locations in the park where she could take her cubs if their security here was compromised. But now it was time, and she settled down to await the arrival of her family.

Raat-ki-Rani gave birth to four lovely cubs in that cave: the eldest, a boy, who she called Zafraan because of his fiery orange coat, and three girls—Hasti, Masti and Phasti.

Hasti was a fat rollicking little thing, tumbling about happily and seemingly only interested in her mother's milk bar, Masti had the gleam of mischief in her frosty blue eyes from the moment she opened them. Poor Phasti, the littlest of the litter, had actually got stuck inside her Mamma before she popped out, and now stumbled and tripped about in the cave, getting herself stuck between rocks and entangling her tail in tree roots; she seemed to have a co-ordination problem. She had gorgeous jade green eyes, the colour of a mountain stream. Masti had a huge amount of fun at her expense.

For the first few weeks their mother rarely ventured out, only setting forth to hunt when she was ravenous. The cubs were happy guzzling her milk and matters at the milk bar often degenerated into quarrels and quibbling.

'Oof fatso, move over!' Masti nudged Hasti, who giggled and promptly squashed Zafraan as she wriggled aside to make room for her sister.

'Mamma, look at her!' Zafraan wailed. 'She's squashing me and not letting me drink!'

Little Phasti, at the very end of the queue, just closed her eyes and drank as fast as she could before she got pushed away by the others.

'Okay, that's enough, all of you,' Raat-ki-Rani stood up as the cubs fell over protesting. 'Mamma, we're still hungry!'

'So am I,' their mother growled, stretching. Very gently she licked them one by one. 'Now stay here quietly, till I get back!'

They were obedient little tiger cubs, at least until they were about four or five weeks old. That's when Masti got the urge to explore and promptly infected her sisters and brother with the bug. Early one morning they waited for their mother to set forth, very innocently crouching at the back of the cave until she had left.

'Come on, kiddos, let's go!' Masti said, her blue eyes sparkling. 'Mamma's gone! The coast is clear!' She led the way to the mouth of the cave and stuck her head out.

'OMG!' she whispered. 'You have got to see this!'

For a while they just sat there side by side at the entrance of the cave, taking in the view of the place which was their home.

'Wow! Just look at that!' Hasti stared, amazed. 'Awesome!'

'I think one day I will be boss of all this,' Zafraan said pompously.

'Oh yeah, sure it will!' Masti said, pouncing on her brother. 'Come on Hasti, let's flatten him!' Hasti joined in and in a moment the cubs were tumbling about, yarring and yowling as they played. Then poor Phasti got swiped by one of her sisters and tumbled down the first two rock steps and got caught in a cleft at the bottom of the second step.

'Help!' she wailed, struggling to get out. 'I'm stuck!'

'Story of her life!' Masti giggled, looking down at her, as Hasti rolled over laughing.

'You girls!' Zafraan sneered, lying down and crossing his paws. 'Such juveniles!'

Hasti nudged Masti. 'He's been reading *The Jungle Book* by Rudyard Kipling, so thinks he's very smart. Mamma said that fellow made the tiger, Sher Khan, the villain of his story!'

'What a douche-bag! We'd show him, wouldn't we?'

'Help!' yowled Phasti, struggling in vain. 'Stop yakking and get me out of here!'

'Really,' Masti said, shaking her head and taking aim at Zafraan's wiggling tail. 'All these humans are the same—they think they are very brave if they shoot us from half a mile away while sitting up on an elephant or from a treetop. Let them come after us on foot, naked and bare-handed!'

'Naked!' Hasti giggled. 'We'll probably run away if we see a naked human. They're hairless and gross! Ugh!'

'Ouch!' Zafraan yelped, leaping up as Masti landed on his tail and worried it. 'Cut that out!'

A large cross-shaped shadow suddenly passed swiftly over them, accompanied by a whistling sound. Diclo, the critically endangered white-backed vulture whizzed by, his eyes raking the little cubs, followed by his wife, Fenac.

'Run!' Masti squealed. 'Get inside!'

The three cubs dived back into their cave.

'What the hell was that?' Hasti asked weakly.

'A pair of white-rumped or white-backed vultures,' Zafraan informed them. 'They've nearly been wiped out... *Gyps bengalensis*!'

'Hey, where's Phasti?' Masti looked around.

'Shoot, she's still stuck!'

'Oh heck, Mamma will kill us if anything happens to her...'

Cautiously they poked their heads out of the cave and then belly-crawled out. A terrifying sight met their eyes. Two steps down, sitting on either side of a petrified Phasti were the two enormous vultures, their bald heads gleaming. They were regarding poor little Phasti in an interested sort of way.

'We'll have to kill it, can't wait till it dies; its mother'll come back!' Diclo croaked.

'Yeah, though I prefer them dead for a couple of days. Nice and tender they become then.'

'...and garnished with bluebottles and maggots. Yum!'

'Come on, we peck its eyes first?'

'I guess!'

Masti didn't hesitate. With a yowl of rage she leapt at the enormous birds startling them. 'Get away from her, you ghouls!' she screamed. Hasti leapt after her and Zafraan, trying to (unsuccessfully) growl deep in his throat, followed in a more dignified manner. They sat around their little sister, growling and swiping their paws at the two huge birds that had skipped away.

'Look at them!' Diclo said.

'Little wildcats, eh?' Fenac added. She lunged towards Hasti, who screeched and snarled.

'What a little tempest!' Diclo grinned. He glanced up. 'Ah,' he said, 'the squadron's arrived!' Four more enormous shadows swept across the rock-face and suddenly the little tiger cubs were confronted by half a dozen (extremely rare, it has to be said) white-rumped and long-billed vultures. It certainly didn't bode well for them.

At the base of the rock-face, Raat-ki-Rani looked up at the wheeling birds. They were settling very close to her cave and cubs. She tightened her grip on the delicious wild boar she had killed, and leapt lithely up the rocks towards her cave. A terrible sight met her eyes when she reached the rock where Phasti was stuck. Her three other babies were squatting in a semi-circle in front of the trapped cub, swiping valiantly at six enormous ugly birds, who were openly laughing as they lunged and thrust their hideous faces and beaks towards them, squawking harshly. Raat-ki-Rani dropped the boar and with a low growl leapt like a flame from a flamethrower. As one, the birds jumped off the cliff face, unfurled their enormous wings and wheeled away.

'What did you do that for? We were just having some fun!' Diclo whined petulantly as he swept around.

'You stay away, you diseased bats from hell!' the angry tigress snarled. Then she turned to her cubs.

'All of you okay?' she demanded, gently lifting Phasti out of the cleft.

'Sure Mamma, we're good,' Masti said cheekily.

'I told you to stay in the cave! So what were you doing outside?'

'It was her idea,' Masti pointed to Hasti who pointed to Phasti who pointed to Masti. Zafraan smirked.

'Such juveniles,' he sneered, 'really!'

Their mother looked at them balefully. She knew it would be impossible to keep them confined to the cave much longer—they were growing up so fast! It would be better if she took them around and began teaching them the ways of the jungle and how to live in it.

'Very well,' she said, 'lessons will start immediately!' She retrieved the wild boar and ripped it open. The cubs stared at it, licking their lips.

'Okay, help yourselves. Normally you'll have to take the hair and skin off, but I'll do it for you this time. The rear parts are the softer ones and you must always go for the organs first because they're good for you... Now, mind your manners!'

Their table manners were, frankly speaking, quite

disgraceful as they clambered all over the tough boar, trying to get to grips with it.

Down in the meadows, the beautiful Ayesha, out on her rounds, had been following the flight of the Diclo-Fenac squadron and photographing them. They were critically endangered birds, after all. She watched as they landed on the cliff face and then her mouth dropped open in astonishment as they teased the cubs.

'Tiger cubs!' She focused her lens on them, even as Raat-ki-Rani leapt up gracefully and charged at the birds.

Ayesha shook her jet black tresses as the tiger family disappeared inside the cave. 'I don't believe it,' she whispered incredulously. 'She has cubs! They're adorable!'

Of course, Diclo and Fenac couldn't keep their mouths shut. Before long, all the hyenas and jackals and tigers in the park knew that Raat-ki-Rani had had a litter of four cubs.

'Huzoor, you are the proud father of four splendid cubs!' Naradmunni informed Shaan-Bahadur, stretching himself prostrate. The macho tiger eyed him like he was some kind of vermin.

'So what's so great about that?' he sneered.

'Three are girl cubs and one a boy cub...'

'*Three* girls? Pah!' The magnificent tiger grimaced and spat. 'I want to have nothing to do with them!'

'You don't have to, huzoor. The gorgeous Begum Raat-ki-Rani is bringing them up splendidly. They will be a credit to you!'

'Stop disturbing me now...' Shaan-Bahadur yawned and stretched out, unsheathing his claws and carefully examining them. 'I need a manicure!'

🐾

'Hah!' snarled Thug, 'that stupid Shaan-Bahadur can only have little girlies. What kind of genes does he have? Thinks he's a stud!'

'And he struts around as if he owns the show!' Caligua added.

'Three girls? Did you say *three* girls?' Razia smirked maliciously. 'Oh my word, poor Rani!'

'And they say the boy is bit of a...a...well, not boy enough...' Resham added with great satisfaction. 'He likes reading...'

'With three sisters, what can you expect?'

'We must extend our good wishes—and sympathies of course—to dear Rani... But three girls...' The tigresses dissolved into giggles.

3

'Mamma, what's a poacher?'
'What's a man-eater?'
'What's a zoo?'
'Who's our Papa?'
'Who was Jim Corbett?'
'Hey, I asked first!'
'I did!'
'Did not!'
'Did too!'
'Did not!
'I'll show you!'

Within seconds a spirited rough and tumble wrestling bout was going on in the cave as the cubs launched themselves at each other.

'Just look at them, Mamma,' Zafraan said, settling down under his mother's chin and watching the scrimmage. 'Little hooligans!'

'Girls, did you hear that?' Masti paused and turned,

her ice-blue eyes sparkling. 'Little Lord Fauntleroy called us hooligans!'

'Gettim babes!'

'Mamma, help! You ghouls—stay away! Mamma, tell them!'

Raat-ki-Rani licked her son and purred affectionately. 'Okay girls, break it up...'

'So Mamma, what's a poacher?'

'Now stop climbing all over me and sit down and I'll tell you.' With Zafraan still claiming pride of place under his mother's chin, the other three arranged themselves around her expectantly.

'A poacher is one of those two-legged hairless cowards who will kill you if he can. He might use any revolting method he can think of—poison, traps or guns.'

'But why?' Masti asked, her eyes wide. 'What have we done to them?'

'For many reasons, but nowadays because millions of hairless and brainless cowards think that by making "medicines" out of our bones they will become less cowardly and maybe more like us. Also, our skins are in great demand...' An angry glint entered her eye, 'and are made into rugs and cloaks. They also hang our heads on the walls of their houses.'

'What's with them?' Hasti shook her head, truly horrified. 'Are they sick?'

'Well dear, in the past the hairless cowards used to

think that they were very brave if they hunted us. So they came after us with guns and elephants and beaters. Then the fools realized that there were so few of us left that we might disappear altogether, so they tried to stop the slaughter.' She snorted. 'Typical, first they cause a problem then they run around chasing their tailless bottoms trying to set it right when it gets out of control!'

'Sounds like Phasti,' Masti said and Hasti giggled.

'Actually...' Zafraan said smirking, 'those hairless creatures reproduce quicker than rabbits and then they have no place to live so they push and shove and fight each other and enter our territory...'

'God, what a pathetic species!'

'And Mamma, what's a man-eater?'

Raat-ki-Rani nodded. 'It's a tiger that likes to kill and eat those hairless creatures.' She grimaced. 'Either these tigers are cowards because it's just so easy to kill them, or usually there's something wrong with them and they can't hunt properly. Either way they're trouble... Once they start, they get addicted.'

'Yes,' Zafraan said, nodding his head sagely. 'And then the hairless ones set people like Jim Corbett after them and all of us get a bad name. Like that Kipling fool gave us...'

'Who's Corbett?' Hasti asked.

Zafraan shook his head witheringly. 'God, don't you read? You don't know who Corbett is? He used to hunt man-eaters on foot…killed a huge number of them… Those hairless creatures loved him.'

Hasti's eyes gleamed. 'I'm going to be a man-eater when I grow up,' she decided. Her mother slapped her gently.

'Baby, you are not!'

Masti stretched languidly and licked her coat. 'Actually I think I already am,' she smirked. Then she frowned. 'But Mamma, when I looked at myself in the pool this morning I thought I saw zits…'

'Those were bluebottles, sweetie, you didn't wash up properly after eating!'

'Oh, thank God, I nearly fainted when I saw them!'

Hasti grinned and nudged Phasti. 'Masti spends most of her time looking at herself in the pool…'

'Do not!'

'Do too!'

Hasti winked. 'Next time we see her doing that, we'll push her in!'

'Dare you!' Masti growled. 'Besides, that one…' she pointed to poor Phasti, 'she'll probably fall in all by herself!'

'So why are you worried then?'

Another scrimmage broke out. Zafraan looked at his mother.

'Girls!' he snorted shaking his head. 'No sense at all!'

His mother purred. And you, my snooty little beta-jaan, she thought, you are just like your father. A burra sahib from the word go!

But she had to admit that the cubs' father Shaan-Bahadur had both style and substance...

Phasti wriggled free from her sisters' clutches and jumped on to her mother's head.

'Mamma, who's our Papa?' she asked.

Raat-ki-Rani sighed. 'Okay you two, break it up and listen.'

With Zafraan still under her chin, and Phasti settled comfortably on top of her massive head making faces at her sisters, the tigress took the plunge. It was time the cubs knew about their father.

'Your father is Rana Shaan-Bahadur—the boss tiger of the park!'

'Wow!'

'Not only that, he's world famous! His pictures have appeared on television and in newspapers and magazines in every country of the world. He's said to be the only tiger in the world to have caught poachers in their own trap.'

'But Mamma, why hasn't he come to see us?' Phasti asked in a small voice. 'He hasn't come even once or brought us presents or anything.'

Raat-ki-Rani swallowed. Good question, sweetheart, she thought. Why hadn't the fellow even bothered to check on his family even once? Surely he knew about the cubs; word got around here very quickly. What a pompous oaf. Just because he had become a celebrity didn't mean he could ignore his family. He must be running after some bimbo, that flirty airhead Lolita, for instance. She growled softly deep in her throat.

'Baby, your father is a very busy tiger with a lot of responsibilities. He has to make sure all the other tigers stay in their territories and behave themselves.'

'But we want to meet him.'

'Tell you what,' their mother said with a sigh. 'He loves posing for photographers on the ramparts of the Sher-kila at sunrise and sunset, so one morning, if he's there, I'll take you along and you can see him.'

'Great!'

'Can I get his autograph?' Phasti asked, her green eyes shining.

'We'll see at the time, okay?' her mother replied, twitching her ears.

'You can have mine!' Zafraan offered generously. 'But you'll have to be nice to me!'

'Mamma, will you listen to him!' Hasti said.

'Yes,' Masti grinned, 'his ego's as big as you are!'

'Are you calling me fat?'

'You said the F-word babe, not me!'

'There they go again!' Zafraan remarked.

'Mamma,' Phasti asked, 'so what's a zoo?'

Her mother's thick fur on her ruff rose instinctively. 'Baby, a zoo can be one of the worst places in the world for a tiger or for any animal...'

'But why?' the three sisters chorused.

'I can't believe it! My sisters are such total dodos! They don't know what a zoo is!'

'It's a place where those hairless cowards keep us in cages and then make faces at us like some of the monkeys here do.'

'Why?'

'Well, because they think that not everyone of their kind can actually see us or make faces at us in the jungle... so they trap us and cage us.'

'That's just so weird!'

'Do they feed the tigers in a zoo?'

'Of course! Zoo tigers don't have to hunt. Also, some of the cages can be pretty comfortable, or so I've heard. In some places they even have something called air-conditioning...' Raat-ki-Rani shook her head, 'but it's still no place for any self-respecting tiger or tigress!'

'I wouldn't mind having meals served to me, and air-conditioning,' Hasti mused. 'And no hunting...wow! A life of leisure.'

'It'll kill your soul; you'll go mad and pace up and down your cage a million times a day, not even knowing that you are doing that! Just hope you never know what a cage is.'

Zafraan shook his head. 'I heard that in some places they have enclosures for tigers which have glass walls so that if the tigers want to do "it" they have to in front of everyone. How sick is that!'

'Do what?' Masti asked innocently.

'Tell us, bro!'

'The gory details! We want the gory details, your lordship!' Hasti giggled.

'You girls are beyond help! Mamma, they're crazy!'

'Okay, you lot, let's go for a swim now!'

'Yay, Mamma!'

With great dignity Raat-ki-Rani led her excited family down the rock-face and headed towards a ravine.

'Mamma, why don't we swim in that pool?' Hasti asked, looking towards Magar and Machch's waterhole.

'Because you'll end up as the crocs' dinner, sweetheart! Now follow me.'

They made their way to a quiet hidden pool deep in the ravines where the cubs played and splashed as Raat-ki-Rani cooled off. She half submerged herself in the cool water and relaxed. The cubs were fooling around as usual, racing up and down the banks and splashing into the water, pouncing and jumping. Suddenly they were quiet, and instinctively Raat-ki-Rani opened one eye to check on them. They had gathered in a semi-circle around a large hole at the base of some rocks, cocking their heads this way and that.

'Can't you smell it?' Hasti said, wrinkling up her nose.

Masti peered into the hole. 'Can't see a thing, but it's there. It's making a noise and it stinks. I think it farted!'

'You idiots, get away from there; it may be a snake!' Zafraan said, backing away.

'It's not making a snake-like noise! It's grunting!'

'Wow, might be a wild boar. If we can kill it Mamma will be so proud!'

'Phasti, you're the littlest. See if you can crawl in and check it out!'

'Sure, sure, and get my eyes scratched out!'

Hasti jumped up on to the rock above the hole and bounced up and down on it.

'Shoo, scat! Get out of there!'

'Knock, knock, who's there?' Masti giggled.

Zafraan rolled his eyes and glanced towards his mother.

Just then, there came a terrifying, angry grunting from the hole, followed by a frightening rattling noise!

'Get out of there!' Raat-ki-Rani shrieked, leaping to her feet. In a flash she was beside them, cuffing them away from the hole. Astonished, they tumbled into the water, just as the most terrifying creature, full of spines, reversed out of the hole at a fearsome speed, grunting and roaring. Raat-ki-Rani jumped away from it, her eyes blazing, a deep growl reverberating, her ears flattened back.

'Wha...?'

'Mamma!'

'Stay in the water!'

The creature eyed their mother balefully. 'Madam, you and your filthy pups have dishonoured me, leader of the

Al-Seekh-Kebab Atankvad Aandolan!' it hissed. 'Death to you!' Then he trundled off, rattling his spikes horrifyingly.

Raat-ki-Rani watched him go and then joined her cubs in the water.

'Mamma, what was that?'

'It was a concubine!' Zafraan said smugly. 'They're deadly!'

Raat-ki-Rani nodded. 'Porcupine, not concubine, beta-jaan, but yes equally deadly! Babies, you flushed out a leading member of the ASKAA, the Al-Seekh-Kebab terrorist movement! We're going to have to be very careful in future. They're going to come after us!'

'Who are they?'

'They're a bunch of fundamentalist porcupines who have sworn to convert all tigers into man-eaters so that people will shoot them to extinction.'

'But how will they do that?'

'You saw their quills? Well, they attack us charging backwards and embed as many of those terrible spines into us. Tigers can go lame or blind, or even die. At any rate the injured ones soon take to killing humans because that's so easy. They are then deemed to be man-eaters and shot. So you see how devious they are!'

'But Mamma, why do they want to exterminate us? What have we done to them?'

'Umm, they're very tasty, so we eat them, sometimes. But only a very experienced tiger or tigress is able to kill them without being injured.' Her eyes softened. 'Your father is one of the greatest porcupine hunters of all time. He doesn't get the slightest prick while killing them. In fact he brought me fresh porcupine many times and taught me how to eat them without stabbing myself with the quills.' She sighed. 'Many of them, in fact, were members of ASKAA, and they've sworn to kill him too.'

'One day, I shall be the most famous porcupine killer of them all,' Zafraan averred.

'Sure, sure, Mr. Pincushion,' Hasti said, rolling over with laughter.

'If I recall Mr Hero, you were furthest away from the mouth of the hole,' Masti added.

Raat-ki-Rani regarded her family, immensely relieved. It had been a close call—any one of the cubs could have been horribly impaled by that psycho porcupine.

'Now listen up, all of you; never get anywhere close to those creatures. Being impaled by them means a slow, horrible death. Okay?'

'Sure, Mamma!'

'Okay!'

'And now, something else to cheer you up…'

'What, Mamma?'

'I'm taking you hunting with me tomorrow at first light! You're old enough now and it's time…'

'Wow!'

'At last!'

'Mamma, we love you!'

'Seriously, Mamma, do those three morons have to come along too? Can't they stay behind and do the housework or something?'

'You four will only observe and watch me and do exactly as I say. You will not get in my way or cause any disturbance, is that clear? Or you won't have anything to eat!'

'Sure, Mamma!'

'We'll be good!'

'Like we always are!'

'There goes your hunt, Mamma! And we're going to starve! We'll be eating beetles!'

'Okay, now pack it up and get some rest! Let's go back to the cave!'

'Okay, Mamma!'

🐾

'Revenge!' roared the terrible one-eyed Col. 'Cuddles' Khujlimal, the leader of the Al-Seekh-Kebab Atankvad Aandolan, foaming at the mouth after he had scuttled into the den of his second-in-command and younger brother, Lieutenant Col. Kabab-me-Haddi.

'Revenge shall be ours! I was resting quietly in the headquarters, when the tigers launched an unprovoked attack! I could impale only seven of them before escaping!' He rattled his quills fearsomely.

'All tigers must die!' the Lieutenant Col. agreed.
'Slowly and very painfully!'
'Kill the tigers! Kill the tigers!'
'How do we do it, boss?'

Col. 'Cuddles' nodded slowly. His little eyes pulsed red with cunning and rage.

'Thissss….' he hissed malevolently, 'is what we're going to do…'

Lieutenant Col. Kabab-me-Haddi shook his head awestruck. 'No one can better that plan! And God can only be with us!'

'So he shall! So he shall! He has no choice!'

4

Khoon-Pyaasa sat down gingerly and scowled. Even now, months after the humiliating incident with the trap, his bottom was as pulpy as an overcooked cauliflower. He and his assistant, Pappu, who had been whacked clean out of the water by an over-excited Magar (much to the crocs' chagrin) had fled the waterhole helter-skelter after the appearance of the tiger with Pyaasa holding on to his bum for dear life. They had returned to their village on the outskirts of the park and had become the butt of rude laughter and jokes. But even worse, their pictures were soon flashed all over the world thanks to some nosy photographer. Then the park authorities along with the police had turned up and taken them into custody.

Fortunately, they had been able to obtain bail. They had very influential sponsors in Delhi and the police obviously thought that as a source of endless ridicule they'd be punished more outside jail than inside it. They were right, and Khoon-Pyaasa had grown a beard to hide his identity, and Pappu had shaved his head completely. But Khoon-Pyaasa had sworn to take down the tiger that had done this to him, or well just about any tiger as well as the photographer (and a woman at that!) who had taken the photographs. This time he would wait for that tiger with a gun...

The beautiful Ayesha of the jet black tresses was also getting a bit exasperated. The gorgeous tiger she had photographed and made world famous appeared to be bit of a show-off. She wasn't too keen on prying into his private life any more ('He just eats and sleeps and goes to his beautician and looks at his reflection in the water,' she told herself, 'not a very interesting dude!'). He kept appearing on the ramparts of the Sher-Kila posing statuesquely and causing many breathless young girls to squeal and faint. She'd got enough pictures of him.

What she now wanted was to photograph that gorgeous tigress she had spotted and her lovely little cubs. She knew how dangerous a tigress with cubs could be, so Ayesha kept her distance from the rock-face and ravines where she had spotted them, but kept a steady vigil from a vantage point. Alas, Raat-ki-Rani was too experienced a tigress and Ayesha never caught another glimpse of her or her cubs, simply because the tigress had moved her family to a den deep in some ravines near the eastern boundary of the park, close to a lovely clear stream, some distance behind the spot the photographer had chosen! Poor Ayesha was looking entirely in the wrong direction! If she had only turned around…

Khoon-Pyaasa, however, was an expert tracker and was soon hot on the trail of Shaan-Bahadur. He knew the tiger made an exhibition of himself on the ramparts of the fort, but it was too dangerous to attempt shooting him there. There were simply too many camera-happy tourists and wildlifers around. But yes, this was the spot from where he could track the tiger and follow it when it left the fort. And then…when it was well away from the public's gaze, he'd get it.

Rana Shaan-Bahadur was having issues of his own. Sure, he'd become a celebrity tiger and was being photographed by his adoring fans every time he went up to the fort and strutted around there, but the media appeared no longer interested in him. His TRPs were plummeting. The beautiful photographer who had made him famous had disappeared. Well not quite, because one morning Naradmunni came up to him in a state of great excitement.

'Huzoor, you know that dhimchack camera chick?'

'What dhimchack camera chick?'

'The one with the long black hair who photographed you and made you world famous!'

'What about her?'

'She's putting up at the Forest Rest House near the south-eastern boundary of the park. That's quite close to where the lovely Begum Raat-ki-Rani is bringing up your wonderful family.'

'What the hell is she doing there?'

'According to that disgusting Diclo-Fenac couple she wants to photograph them. So far Her Excellency Raat-ki-Rani has, very correctly, not allowed herself or your babies to be seen or photographed.' Naradmunni closed his eyes. 'Huzoor, it would be so wonderful if you joined them and you all could pose for a family photograph… Imagine the publicity! And…' the jackal's eyes shone, 'if you could ask her to take the cubs up to the fort and pose from there…huzoor, the park will be declared a Heritage Site in no time at all! They'll frame your photograph and put it up at the entrance to the park and rename it the Rana Shaan-Bahadur National Park!'

'Eh? What the hell are you talking about?'

'And you will be a Heritage Tiger! The Tiger First Family of India!'

'Don't talk rubbish. You know I can't be seen nuzzling and cuffing around with cubs like some gaga-goo-goo tigress! My reputation will be like yours! All those other fools, Thug, Caligua and company will roll over laughing. I'll no longer be top tiger!'

Naradmunni lowered his eyes. 'Whatever you say, huzoor! Of course you are right. Forget I ever brought up the subject.'

'Hmm…but something needs to be done if I have to

appear on prime time television again. Maybe I should become a man-eater and make those reality television fellows sit up.'

Naradmunni shook his head in horror. 'Huzoor, forgive my saying so but if you do that the only footage that will be taken of you will be of your head on a pole with crowds singing and dancing and beating drums around it. I know what these hairless humans are like.'

'So do you have any useful suggestions?'

'Sire, the luscious lady Lolita is pining for you! Why don't you romance her on the battlements of the fort? You know, chase her around the battlements and towers and then as the sun sinks behind you in a golden ball of glory... That should make stunning footage.'

'That Lolita plays fast and loose! Necking at every opportunity with any and every moth-eaten fellow that comes her way, and caterwauling all night...quite disgraceful! No dignity! My reputation will be down the tube if I'm seen chasing her!'

'But of course, sire!' Naradmunni looked at the sun. 'Huzoor, it is time for your royal bath and then grooming and then your evening stroll to the ramparts of the fort for another photo-shoot.'

'Pah! What a life!'

'Ah, huzoor, then at dusk we set out hunting. I hear a large flock of tender young chital have moved into the big meadow west of Magar-Machch's waterhole.

Should be easy pickings for you, huzoor. I'll collect some fresh wild parsley, basil and rosemary for garnish. And tomorrow huzoor, at first light you set out for your weekly territorial patrol. There have been rumors that Shri Thug has been trying to sneak in and annex small sections of your northern territories near the kila. It is said that he wishes to be photographed at the kila too.'

'I see, I'll kill him! The slimeball!'

'I shall just make sure everything is in order for your bath and that the water is at the right temperature, huzoor!' Naradmunni bowed, wagged his tail ingratiatingly and trotted off in his usual servile manner.

Suddenly Shaan-Bahadur perked up. He knew exactly how to become the centre of attention again. He'd challenge that slimy Thug to a fight! A fight on the battlements of the Sher-kila! Imagine the publicity that would garner. Two full-grown Royal Bengal tigers battling it out on the battlements as the sun went down behind them in a great ball of glory and then the full moon rose, butter gold! Of course he'd make mincemeat of Thug, no question about that! But this…this would be better than all those nonsensical Rocky films even and certainly better than a soppy soap opera involving the romancing of a disgracefully flirty tigress like Lolita! His ratings would rocket! He really was a genius!

'Naradmunni!' he roared. 'Where the hell are you? Get your slinky butt back here immediately and listen and tremble! The great Rana Shaan-Bahadur has had an idea!'

Naradmunni listened in awe.

'Brilliant, sir, absolutely brilliant, a work of sheer genius!' Naradmunni rolled over on his back in supplication. 'I'll make all the arrangements, sire!'

'Good! Now show me to my bath…'

5

'Come along now, quietly!' Raat-ki-Rani slipped out of the cave and waited for her brood. They were quivering with excitement. Hasti and Masti shoved each other trying to take the lead, Zafraan strolled regally behind his sisters and poor Phasti got her tail stuck in a bush then freed it with a jerk and went tumbling down the rocks.

'Mamma!' she yowled. 'Help!'

Her mother glared at her as the others giggled. 'Okay, now listen up and listen good: We're going after chital. There's a herd very near the waterhole. You four will remain absolutely silent and observe me. I want no interference from any of you, is that clear?'

'Yes, Mamma!'

'Afterwards I expect each of you to describe the hunt to me in complete detail!'

'Mamma, this is like school!'

'It is. Now come along. In single file and quietly!'

Hasti and Masti, of course, continued to shove and

jostle each other in attempts at being at the head of the line, while Zafraan knit his eyebrows and sneered. Poor Phasti struggled to keep up and occasionally her brother would stop and look back and wait till she caught up.

'Thanks,' Phasti panted. 'I keep falling all over myself!'

'You do,' he agreed dryly, 'what to do?'

They climbed down to the base of the rock-face and entered the ravines skirting the stream. They had to tread carefully here and it was all Masti could do not to shove her sister into the water. They soon entered the thick forest beyond. Raat-ki-Rani stopped and crouched, figuring out the direction of the breeze. It was perfect. She could smell the chital in the meadow beyond; the breeze was down wind from them. She crouched down and began the stealthy stalk towards the open meadow. At the edge of the forest, she stopped and assessed the scene ahead of her.

A scattered herd of chital was browsing, occasionally looking up to check if everything was all right. Fortunately there were no langurs or peacocks around, and the chital seemed oblivious of the tigress. A stag and two does and a fawn were drifting towards where the tigress waited, peering from behind the trees. They were fifty metres away when they stopped. A doe looked in their direction, her foot raised, her ears pricked. Raat-ki-Rani froze. Behind her, the cubs sat holding their breath. The doe lowered her foot quietly and resumed browsing. The fawn frolicked heedlessly around the little group, happy to be alive. The cubs watched it and quivered. Raat-ki-Rani crouched down on to her belly and slithered out into the meadow, her orange-gold coat melding into the waving grass.

'Where's Mamma gone?' Hasti murmured, suddenly alarmed.

'She was just there!' Masti was equally puzzled.

'Are you blind? Can't you see her?' Phasti had caught up with her sisters. She could see the outline of her mother's body clearly. 'She's in the grass right in front of us!'

Zafraan nodded. He hadn't spotted his mother but he wasn't going to admit that.

'Those two are blind as bats!' he sneered.

The chital stopped browsing and froze again. Raat-ki-Rani just disappeared in the high grass. The stand-off continued for almost ten minutes before the deer relaxed. Behind her, Raat-ki-Rani could sense the cubs getting fidgety. She would have to launch an attack sooner than she wanted: those four were not going to be able to keep still and silent much longer. She belly-crawled ahead, her blazing eyes riveted on the chital closest to her. The fawn was still bouncing all over the place, blissfully oblivious to the danger. Raat-ki-Rani could have brought it down in no time but she ignored it: it wouldn't fill the stomachs of her or her family. Besides the fine, healthy stag she had targeted was now quite close by. When it was about twenty metres away, she bunched herself up for the assault. From this distance, she could not miss.

At that moment, the fawn bounced to the very edge of the forest, right in front of the cubs. With a squeal of triumph, Hasti and Masti launched themselves at it, as poor Phasti took a tumble and Zafraan began to laugh. The chital herd scattered as if a bomb had exploded amidst them. The stag and doe bolted in different directions, and the fawn blithely bounced after them, putting on a turn of speed that was amazing. Hasti and Masti landed with a thump on their fat tummies, the breath whooshing out of them.

'Oh shoot!'

'Oooof!'

The chital were gone. Raat-ki-Rani shook her head exasperatedly and looked balefully at her cubs.

'Mamma, she pounced first!' Hasti and Masti said simultaneously, pointing at each other. Then they looked towards Phasti, 'and she fell over!'

Raat-ki-Rani said nothing but just glared at her brood.

'Those two!' Zafraan said, sneaking up to his mother and rubbing his face against her chin. 'They're hopeless. You can't do anything with them! As for poor Phasti...'

'They'll learn eventually,' Raat-ki-Rani murmured. 'They'll have to!' She glanced at him. 'And so will you, beta-jaan!'

Some mornings later, Raat-ki-Rani returned from a

solo hunting trip with a struggling fawn in her jaws. She put it down, one massive paw pinning it to the ground. She'd made the cubs go hungry all through the previous day and they were yowling and leaping after frogs and insects in the grass.

'Okay, listen up. I'm going to let this go and you'll have to bring it down.' She shrugged. 'Otherwise you'll go hungry. On the count of ten, ready? One, two, three four, ten! Go get it, babies!'

She released the fawn which bounced high right over Hasti and Masti and skittered away. Hasti and Masti just stared at it and yowled, 'But Mamma you cheated! You didn't count properly! Wait, come back you!'

Phasti, who was very hungry, had focused fiercely on the fawn. Fresh steak, she thought, fresh steak! She brilliantly anticipated its leap and leapt gracefully at it. She was on it in two bounds, bringing it down with a thump. Yarring, she held it down by its slender throat and clung on till the little thing stopped moving. Zafraan's eyes widened. Hasti and Masti stared open-mouthed.

'Well done, baby!' her mother said, lying down nearby, amusement in her eyes. 'Your first kill!'

Hasti and Masti were outraged. 'But Mamma, you cheated! You said ten after four. Five comes after four!'

'That'll teach you to be ready all the time,' their mother said dryly. 'When you hunt you have to be alert at all times.'

Zafraan got lazily to his feet and approached his sister, who was standing over her kill, her green eyes blazing.

'One step closer and I'll kill you!' she hissed, swiping out at him with her paw. 'This is mine!'

'Hey, hey, easy kiddo, I'm your big bro after all...I look out for you!'

'Keep your distance. And you two—you ghouls,' she spat indicating Hasti and Masti who had also started approaching. 'Stay back!'

'But really, that was brilliant!' Zafraan shook his head admiringly. 'How did you know in which direction it was going to jump?'

'Easy,' Phasti allowed herself a grin. 'Even the fawn knew those two fat dopes were dodos so jumping over them was its obvious escape route...so I knew in which direction it was going to bolt!'

'Brilliant. Amazing anticipation! Pure genius!'

Phasti looked pleased. Praise from Zafraan always made her purr and besides he had been the only one who had often waited for her to catch up when their mother took them for walks in the jungle. 'I know,' she said modestly, 'thank you.'

'Could I have the honour of dining with you at your magnificent table?' Zafraan asked, inclining his head. He was drooling already. Phasti glanced at her sisters. It would be difficult to defend 'her magnificent table' from both of them, but with Zafraan at her side it was two against two. And anyway, she wouldn't be able to eat the entire fawn…

'Sure,' she said, inclining her head. 'You're welcome!'

'Thank you!'

His mother glanced at him. You are one sly charmer, beta-jaan, she said to herself. As for Hasti and Masti, they exchanged glances. They were drooling too now, because their siblings had opened up the fawn and were feasting, crunching up bones with evident enjoyment. Masti sighed.

'Some tigers are so ungrateful,' she said with tears in her voice and shaking her head. Hasti nodded.

'Yes, they forget…so quickly.'

'After all, I risked my life by leaping at those horrible vultures. And now…and now…' She choked back a sob.

Hasti controlled a giggle. 'Yes,' she agreed sorrowfully. 'If we hadn't attacked those birds, little Phasti would not have been with us today.'

'Let alone made her first kill.'

'And now, she won't even share it with us…'

'Not even a mouthful…'

Phasti looked at them. She was a tender-hearted little cub. Besides, she had proved her point—she'd made the first kill. She inclined her head.

'Okay, you may have some,' she agreed. 'But no gobbling or running away with a haunch…'

Later, happily reclining under her mother's chin (Zafraan had generously let her have the spot) Phasti snoozed while her mother licked her affectionately.

'Baby, you'll be a good huntress,' she murmured. 'But you've got to toughen up. Otherwise, you're going to be taken advantage of all your life.' She nuzzled her. 'But tell me, how was it that you didn't stumble or trip when you were leaping at the fawn? You jumped clean as a whistle.'

Phasti shook her head. 'Mamma, I think I just forgot to! I was only thinking about how delicious it would be and how hungry I was and that I just had to get it! I didn't think about tripping or stumbling or anything like that.'

'Well done, baby!'

'Thanks, Mamma!'

'Sheer luck!' Masti said to Hasti. 'Sheer luck and nothing more.'

'Yeah, she just happened to be in the right place at the right time.'

'Besides, Mamma cheated.'

'Yes, and she favours her!'

'And that Zafraan had to go and suck up to her.'

'Such a lazy slob.'

'Wait till he has to hunt for himself.'

But in the days that followed, it became clear that little Phasti had the knack of always being in the right place at the right time while hunting. She was best at making herself invisible in the grass and wriggling really close to the prey and she had an uncanny ability to know in which direction the prey would bolt. While on the hunt, she neither tripped nor caught her tail in bushes, nor stumbled, she was indeed graceful as a leopard. Sometimes of course, she got into trouble, when for instance she picked on a young wild boar, which suddenly turned around and charged her. (Fortunately, her mother was nearby and one swipe from her paw settled the issue.) Hasti and Masti didn't seem able to take a hunt seriously, as for Zafraan beta-jaan, he was always sliming his way around his baby sister after she had killed and hardly expended any energy on hunting himself.

Proud of her brood, who were growing wonderfully well, Raat-ki-Rani began bringing them out on to the forest tracks, familiarising them with their home. Her girls would stay with her for maybe two years; Zafraan—if he learned to hunt for himself, would leave the family when he was about eighteen months to mark out his own territory.

'I mean, if all this is Papa's, why should I have to find my own territory?' he asked his mother. 'Won't all this be mine one day?'

'Maybe,' his mother said laconically. 'But not as long as your father's the boss tiger here!'

'Mamma, does he even know about us, let alone care?' Masti asked.

'I mean, we don't even know what he looks like!' Hasti added.

'Is he handsome?' Phasti asked.

'He must be a great hunter,' Zafraan said proudly.

'Yeah, like you!' Hasti grinned.

'I haven't seen or smelt any trace of him for some time now,' their mother said. 'He's probably touring his border outposts, checking on infiltration.'

She was right. Rana Shaan-Bahadur was indeed patrolling his vast territories and had disappeared from sight, having temporarily suspended his appearances at the Sher-kila. Khoon-Pyaasa, bloodthirsty as ever, lost track of him and decided to take his revenge on whichever tiger he first came across. There was also the matter of the photographer who had caused all the trouble and shame, that needed to be settled. It was a matter of honour and prestige. He knew she was still in the park, driving everywhere in her Gypsy, taking more pictures. Then he had a stroke of luck. He learned at which Forest Rest House she was staying.

'Simple! We go there and kill her!' Pappu said. But Khoon-Pyaasa shook his head.

'Not immediately. She will lead us to the other tigers, too. She knows where they are. She takes their pictures. We kill the tiger and then we kill her. If we kill her first, we won't know where the tigers are and there'll be hell of a hullabaloo anyway. Let her find them for us!'

The beautiful raven-haired Ayesha too, it seemed, had

an uncanny knack of tracking down and finding tigers she could photograph. She simply kept her binoculars focused on the Diclo-Fenac Squadron (and an ear out for the alarm call of peacocks), knowing that they would eventually lead her to a kill.

Early one afternoon, she followed the flight of the squadron; one by one the great birds wheeled down out of the sky and settled heavily on a tree at the edge of a ravine. She drove her Gypsy quietly to the spot and peered into the ravine. A clear silver-blue stream curled through the rocks, tinkling into large pools.

Ayesha gasped and gripped her binoculars tightly, hardly daring to believe what she was seeing. A family of tigers—a mother and four cubs—was reclining in and around the pool; the tigress lying chin deep in the water, the cubs splashing around as they played. Nearby, the skeleton of a nearly completely eaten wild boar glimmered and shimmered with bluebottles.

'I've found you!' Ayesha whispered. 'At last! You're beautiful and what a lovely family you have!'

Alas, she too had been tracked and followed... Pedalling furiously along the tyre tracks of her Gypsy was Khoon-Pyaasa, hot on her trail. He winced as the cycle bounced over the ruts and he stood up in the saddle to protect his still tender bum from the jolts. It is not possible to go very fast in the jungle in a motor vehicle, there are just too many distractions and Ayesha was constantly stopping to take photographs of this and that, so Khoon-Pyaasa really didn't have much of a problem keeping up with her. He saw the Gypsy parked beneath the tree and disembarked from his bicycle, some distance away. Then he peered down into the ravine, to see what she was looking at and photographing so avidly…

6

All that afternoon and evening, Ayesha photographed the family of tigers. With delight she watched the cubs play, mock fight and pretend to hunt each other. She watched Zafraan sidle up to his mother and settle down beneath her chin; she watched the others rough and tumble all over their mother; she saw Raat-ki-Rani lovingly groom her cubs. Occasionally, the tigress would glance up at her, but she didn't seem upset by her presence. Very cautiously, and step by step, Ayesha began descending into the ravine, so that she could get closer. Raat-ki-Rani watched her and gave a low growl when she thought she had come close enough. Ayesha stopped and hunkered down. From this spot she'd get some gorgeous pictures, especially since the sun was turning the animals to pure gold.

Eventually the sun slipped behind some craggy outcrops, and the ravine lay deep in shadow. Ayesha knew it was time to return—being close to a tigress with cubs in the dark was not wise. Thrilled with her pictures, she climbed up the ravine and drove off in her Gypsy, her heart singing.

From behind a huge lantana bush, Khoon-Pyaasa watched her go. He had scanned the ravine thoroughly, walking up and down its length from the top. The walls were almost sheer, impossible for anything or anyone but a mountaineer to climb up. There was only one narrow winding path leading into and out of it, which Ayesha had used and along which the tigers would have to walk to get out and return to the forest. It would be so easy.

Twenty minutes later he shot Raat-ki-Rani clean through the head as she led her family around a narrow bend flanked by high rocks. He'd shimmied up a convenient tree and it was the perfect spot for an assassin. The tigress was flung backwards by the impact of the bullet, but landed on her feet. Then, eyes blazing she roared and charged. Fifteen feet high on his branch, Khoon-Pyaasa yelped with terror and wet his pants. The furious tigress gathered herself for her leap, and as she became airborne, died. But the momentum of her leap enabled her to rake Khoon-Pyaasa's bottom with her claws. With a shout of fright he fell out of the tree and landed on the back of the dead tigress. Somehow he gathered himself, frantically got on to his bicycle and gibbering with terror like a monkey, rattled off at top speed. His bum was going to be very sore for a long time.

The cubs had instinctively bolted and scattered at the

sound of the shot. Hasti and Masti had fled back down into the ravine, and Phasti just vanished headfirst into the nearest lantana bush. Zafraan leapt up at the rock-face, fell back and followed his sisters into the ravine.

Khoon-Pyaasa did not stop cycling till he reached his village.

'Oye, what happened to your bum this time?' Pappu inquired, 'and your pants are all torn.' He raised his eyebrows. 'I don't think you'll be sitting down for a long time now.'

'That tigress! She attacked me after I shot her! I had to flee for my life.'

'Did you kill her?' Pappu tore up a bedsheet and gleefully emptied half a bottle of tincture iodine onto it.

'Yes! Shot her through the head. Owww! Abbe, what the hell are you doing?'

'Hold still! And the cubs?'

'They fled. They'll die. They'll starve without their mother.'

'We should retrieve her body. We'll get a good price for her skin and bones.'

'I'm not going back there—you go! My bum is torn to shreds and I can't even sit down.' He glanced at his bum. 'What the hell have you done, tied a pugree on it?'

'Bandage,' Pappu said succinctly. 'You'd better not fart.'

An hour after the terrible shot had been fired, Hasti, Masti, Phasti and Zafraan, who had found each other in the ravine, padded up the path and approached their mother cautiously.

'That noise!' Hasti complained. 'My ears are still ringing! What was it?'

'Mamma did a backward somersault!' Masti giggled. 'Did you see?'

'Gave me the fright of my life!'

Zafraan shook his head. 'That was a shot. Someone shot at us!'

'Just look at Mamma!' Hasti said. 'She's gone to sleep!'

'Mamma's the limit!'

'What a time to have a snooze!'

'Mamma, wake up! Why are you sleeping here?'

They came up to their mother and nudged and nuzzled her.

'Mamma, wake up!'

'She's bleeding!' Zafraan said suddenly. 'Can't you smell it?'

'Mamma?'

'Wake up!'

'She's not moving!'

'Her eyes are open!'

'But she hasn't seen us!'

'Yoo-hoo Mamma, we're here!'

'Let's get out of here; it's scary!'

'We can't. Not without Mamma!'

They nudged their motionless, silent mother and nuzzled her, clambered all over her, whimpering and mewing. Then they looked at each other, trembling.

'We'll stay here till she wakes up,' Phasti said in a small voice. 'Let's go to sleep with her.'

It was going to be a long night.

Two hours later, the cubs were awakened by a horrible liquid giggling sound.

'Hee-yuck, hee-yuck! Just look at them! So sweet!'

'Cutie pies!'

The cubs opened their eyes and whirled around. From the gloom of the trees they saw glowing pinpoints of green light; and then the gleam of jaws and teeth, glistening with saliva and foam-flecked pink tongues. Four hyenas lurched out of the darkness like apparitions in a nightmare.

'Wh…who…are you and what do you want?' Zafraan asked bravely.

'Your lordship, they call us the Gigglers, do you know why?'

Suddenly the darkness was filled with a most malevolent giggling; it made the fur on the backs of the cubs' necks rise; it made them shiver with fear, a fear that was sharp and icicle cold.

'Now you know…' went on the wheedling voice. 'What we want is to dine on this delicious-looking fresh tigress—your former mother!' The hyena inclined his head towards Raat-ki-Rani and went on: 'So if you will excuse us and get the hell out of here and let us eat in peace!'

The hyenas moved forward menacingly, joined by four others.

'Stay away from Mamma!' Phasti screeched and launched herself at the brute nearest to her. He giggled and turned to flee and she clamped her jaws hard on his tail. He yelped, while the others just rolled about in paroxysms of giggles. Phasti suddenly found her mouth full of bushy, smelly hyena-tail, while the animal fled yelping. She spat it out in disgust.

'She's de-tailed you! Hyuck-hyuck!' A chorus of giggles rippled out into the night air.

'Dum-katta! Dum-katta! Dum-katta!' the hyenas giggled maniacally. But even as they giggled the animals lowered their heads and hunched their backs even more and moved towards the cubs.

'Heeyuck-heeyuck, and babies, we're going to take your heads off with one bite!'

'Come on!' Zafraan snapped, rounding up his sisters like he had never done before. 'Let's get the hell out of here.'

'But Mamma!' Hasti protested.

'We can't desert her!' Masti agreed, looking back. Already the filthy animals were swarming all over their mother, giggling in that blood-curdling way of theirs, their jaws making terrifying crunching sounds. 'Look what they're doing to her!'

'We're never going to see Mamma again,' Zafraan said, trying to quell a rising sob. 'She's gone. A shot through the head! Fatal! I saw the bullet hole!' He gulped.

'What?' the sisters chorused, shocked.

'We'd better go as far away from here as possible. It's too dangerous to stay here.'

'But…' Bleakly Hasti, Masti and Phasti looked back towards where they had left their beloved Mamma.

Weary and whimpering, and still not fully understanding the enormity of what had happened, they followed Zafraan as he led the way back to their current cave hideout at the base of a cliff face.

'We'll stay here for a while and then move out,' he said heavily. 'Those hyenas will be after us.'

Phasti looked around the cave. 'It feels weird without Mamma. I don't like it! I don't want to stay here. I want Mamma!'

'Zafraan, but what are we going to do?' Hasti looked panic-stricken.

'Mamma did everything for us!'

'How'll we eat?'

'I want to go back to see if she's all right.'

'Phasti, Mamma's never going to be all right!' Zafraan said, going up to his sister and licking her face.

'I don't believe you! I bet she'll come walking through the entrance at first light. We dreamt about all those hideous hyena things...'

'Will you please take care of her?' Zafraan asked Hasti and Masti in a choked voice. Silently the two nodded and cuddled up to their little sister.

'We'll look after you, baby,' Hasti said, 'don't worry.'

'Now try to sleep.'

Eventually Phasti did fall asleep, between her two sisters. They looked at each other bleakly.

'We'll look after her...' Hasti said in a tearful voice, 'but who'll look after us?'

Outside, at the entrance to the cave, Zafraan lay down, crossed his paws and grieved silently for his mother.

No human being had either heard, or taken note of the single shot that had rung out late that evening in the ravine, taking down Raat-ki-Rani. The Gigglers gorged themselves all night and lurched away from the remnants of the animal at first light. Later in the morning, from high up, Diclo and his wife Fenac were quick to spot the carcass of the tigress... They went down. Within minutes the news was everywhere.

'Did you hear?' Lolita yowled, completely shocked as she rushed up to the other tigresses who were deciding their respective hunting blocks for the following month. 'Someone shot Raat-ki-Rani last evening and those bloody Gigglers have already torn her apart and eaten most of her!'

'They're so revolting those hyenas—they make you

sick! But she had cubs! I wonder where they are!' Resham's amber eyes shone.

'Wherever they are, they're good as dead!'

'Good riddance!' That was sweet Razia. 'Now I can have mine in peace!'

Rana Shaan-Bahadur had reached the northern-most parts of his territory when the news reached him. Naradmunni suddenly came running up, his head lowered, his tail well between his legs.

'Huzoor, I have heard grave news,' he said with downcast eyes, but flicking a glance sideways for an escape route in case the great tiger decided to get after the messenger of bad tidings.

'What?' Shaan-Bahadur asked irritably. 'We know that Thug has been intruding into my territory and I have challenged him to a fight on the ramparts of the Sher-kila on the night of the coming full moon. That should up my TRP ratings considerably. Make sure all the photographers and press are informed, especially that one with the beautiful tresses.'

'Certainly, huzoor! But, huzoor, I have just heard that the beautiful Begum Raat-ki-Rani has been ruthlessly gunned down by a poacher. As you know, she had four young cubs—your cubs. No one knows where they've gone! They haven't been seen since the shooting.'

'So the bastards nailed her, eh? Really, she ought to have been more careful!'

'But huzoor, the cubs...'

'What about them?'

'They're very young. They'll die without their mother...'

'What's that to do with me?'

'But huzoorji, forgive my saying so, you are their sire! They have your genes!'

'And I am telling you once and for all, I will have nothing to do with them. There will be lots of other cubs carrying my genes, along with the genes of mothers who have better sense than to get themselves shot by a poacher! Look at me. I caught the stinking poacher in his own trap! Hah!' He shook his head. 'Just what was she thinking?'

'Whatever you say, huzoor!'

Ayesha was utterly heartbroken when she heard the news about the killing of Raat-ki-Rani, late the next morning.

'It can't be true!' she wept. 'That gorgeous tigress! I photographed her with her cubs all of last afternoon and evening... Those poor cubs! They'll die without their mother. They were such a loving family! And...and they knew I was there and let me photograph them to my heart's content and never snarled at me even once. They made me feel at home with them. They were like family! My own family!'

And so, again in no time at all, Raat-ki-Rani and

her cubs became Sher-kila National Park's latest, though tragic, international celebrities as their photographs were published around the world.

'We have to find those cubs and help them survive!' Ayesha begged the park authorities. 'Just look what those wretched hyenas did to that beautiful animal!'

'Ma'am, what we do to them is worse,' the Field Director of the park said sephulchrally. 'Don't forget she was shot by a human being. If he had got his way, he would have skinned her or taken her bones and sold them to the Chinese.'

'Yes, I know. Do you have any idea about who may be behind this?'

The swarthy man pushed back his hat and nodded. 'We have ideas, but no proof. We can't move without proof.'

'And the cubs?'

He nodded. 'We will look for them. Trackers will set forth on elephant back to look for them. Once we find them, we'll decide what needs to be done.'

'Thank you. Can I accompany one of the search parties?' Ayesha begged making such big puppy eyes at the Field Director there was no way he could refuse. 'They were like my own family!'

'But of course, ma'am. I'll give instructions.'

'Thank you.'

But in the days that followed, the search parties which fanned out all across the park came across no trace of the orphaned cubs. They had just vanished off the face of the earth.

🐾

Wheeling about, high in the sky, Diclo and Fenac were also looking out for the cubs.

'They're small and young and inexperienced and tender. They'll starve and weaken...'

'And then we move in!' Fenac giggled. 'They got away the first time, but not again...'

There was just one hitch. Even the vultures, with their wonderful telescopic vision and keen sense of smell could find no trace of the cubs.

'They must have died and rotted away!' Razia said with some relish as she came across Lolita while on patrol. 'Besides which, madam step back, you are about to infringe into my territory...'

'If they'd rotted those damn vultures would have spotted them. And I'm on my side of the border if you please!'

'They say that Shaan-Bahadur couldn't give a damn. Didn't even twitch his tail when he heard the news,' Razia snorted. 'Apparently he said something about his cubs needing to have better genes than from a female like Raat-ki-Rani who got herself shot by a poacher. So it was like good riddance.'

'I hear Shaan-Bahadur challenged your stud Thug to

a fight,' Lolita said maliciously.

'He's not my stud for your information. He's just time pass!' But she closed her eyes and purred. 'Still, who knows...'

'Oh yeah, sure, sure! Well wish him best of luck! He'll need it!'

Rana Shaan-Bahadur had just completed clearly marking his territory's northern border—which that coward Thug had intruded into—when Naradmunni trotted up to him again, his face expressionless. He'd know what expression to put on once he gauged his boss's reaction to the news.

'Huzoorji, I hear that the cubs have vanished.'

'Cubs? What cubs?'

'Your cubs, sirji. I mean yours and Begum Raat-ki-Rani's cubs...'

'So?'

'I just thought you ought to know, sire...'

'Well, now I do. Good, if they've vanished. Now can we get on with our lives for a change and not be bothered about what's happening to them?'

'But of course, huzoor. Whatever you say!' He blinked and swallowed. 'Um...huzoor, there's one more thing...'

'Now what?'

'You know that beautiful photographer who made you famous? Ayesha, of the silky black tresses.'

'Yes, what about her?'

'Well huzoor, now she's made Begum Raat-ki-Rani and her cubs world famous too. Apparently she photographed them on the day the Begumji was killed. Their pictures were splashed all over the world! They've gone supercalifragalistichyperviralonthenet.'

'What?' Shaan-Bahadur roared. 'What the hell are you saying?'

'Indeed huzoor, they had better ratings than even you did in your heyday!' Naradmunni wisely scuttled twenty feet away and was poised to flee.

'What? No one, I repeat no one gets better ratings than I do!'

'Of course, huzoor, of course! It must have been a computing error.'

Shaan-Bahadur's green eyes glowed like emeralds. 'And,' he growled so menacingly that poor Naradmunni piddled a little, 'if we ever come across those cubs, I will kill them without hesitation! Stealing my thunder like that! What's this shameless new generation coming to? No respect for their elders! Better ratings than mine? Pah!'

'Thank god they've vanished,' Naradumunni squeaked and then bit his lip. Fortunately his boss was pacing up and down so agitatedly he didn't hear him. 'But of course, huzoor,' he said now, nodding virtuously. 'I'll send the word out that you're looking for them.'

'You do that!'

The cubs had 'vanished' for a very simple reason. For days after their mother's assassination they stayed put in the cave that had been their last nursery. They emerged at dusk to hunt mice and frogs and whatever tidbits they could find; it was dangerous as this was when many big carnivores—tigers, leopards, hyenas and bears set out hunting, so they had to be extremely careful. But it was safer than emerging in the day, when the eyes of the Diclo-Fenac squadron missed nothing. Also, humans went around in daylight and they were the most lethal of all.

'We can't go on like this,' Zafraan decided some days later. 'We're hardly eating. We'll have to get away from here.'

'Do you know for where?' Phasti asked.

'It doesn't matter where. Just far away from here.'

'We're hungry!' Hasti and Masti complained.

'I miss Mamma,' Phasti said tearfully. 'I miss her like anything!'

Zafraan went up to her and licked her comfortingly. 'We miss her too kiddo, but don't worry I'll look after you!'

'My! My!' Hasti smirked in spite of herself. 'Wow! Suddenly we've got such a loving big brother to take care of us! He called her kiddo!'

'Let him try that with me,' Masti snorted. 'He'll get a swipe for his trouble. Kiddo indeed! He's just ensuring she'll share her kills with him, the lazy slob!'

By the fifth night all of them were thinking of just one thing: their nearly empty tummies.

'I'm famished!' Hasti panted.

'I'm starving!' Masti agreed.

'We'll die if we don't eat soon.'

Zafraan looked at his sisters. 'We leave tonight!'

Biting back their tears, they left their nursery for the last time that night, remembering all the fun and games (and magnificent meals) they had had there with their mother. Zafraan led the way, followed by Hasti and Masti, with little Phasti huffing and puffing and tripping and falling as she brought up the rear. Every now and then the little procession would halt to enable the little cub to catch up. They travelled by night and took shelter by day under rocky overhangs or beneath lantana bushes. On the fourth night, they stumbled into an empty cave; it was rather like one of their earlier nurseries, a cave halfway up a rock-face, overlooking a grassy meadow.

Exhausted, they lay down, their eyes sunken, their faces gaunt. They hadn't eaten properly since their mother had died. Zafraan looked sadly at his sisters.

'We'll have to hunt for ourselves. Proper big game! Not rats and bandicoots! There's no other way. Try to remember everything Mamma taught us about hunting…'

Alas, their first attempt was a complete fiasco. They had targeted an experienced chital hind, who detected them very early, snorted derisively and trotted off just out of range. She kept moving away as the cubs valiantly crawled towards her. 'Come closer, come closer and kiss me!' the wretched deer sang, grinning as the rest of the herd looked on in amusement. After a bit the cubs gave up and went back to their cave hideout to discuss the matter.

'Really, you move like a bulldozer!' Hasti accused Masti indignantly.

'Me?' Masti squawked. 'Who tripped over that branch and fell flat on her tummy and squealed like a pig? The whole world must have heard that.'

'You two, you have to learn to move quietly,' Zafraan said in his smarmy voice.

'Look who's talking, bhai-jaan. Who fell into the stream with a splash like a buffalo?'

Then one by one they looked at little Phasti who was sitting quietly, her green eyes sad. She had got closest to the deer, much closer than the others and the animal had been startled by her. And amazingly, she had slunk up close soundlessly, neither tripping on branches nor stepping on crisp, dried leaves.

'I have an idea,' Phasti said quietly. 'Maybe it would work!'

'What's your idea, little girl?' Zafraan asked kindly in that tone that automatically made the claws of his other two sisters unsheathe silently.

'This is what I thought...'

Zafraan listened gravely as Phasti told her plan and then inclined his head regally. 'Yes, excellent, little lady. In fact I was thinking just the same thing! We can try it!'

'What a fibber!' Hasti nudged Masti. 'He just can't stomach the fact that Phasti thought of it. Little lady! Sheesh!'

'Guys, I tell you! Farts, from head to toe!'

They spent the day in their cave hideout fine-tuning Phasti's plan and trying to ignore their rumbling tummies. They had managed to survive on mice, frogs and lizards but that's no diet for growing tiger cubs. As dusk fell, they set out, lithely leaping between and over the rocks. Ahead, where the thorny bush gave way to the grassy meadow, a herd of chital browsed peacefully in the moonlight, some of the animals were even lying down and resting.

Phasti's eyes shone and she checked out the herd. 'Okay,' she whispered to her brother, who was regarding her indulgently. 'That one is the target...' She'd picked a medium-sized doe which was grazing peacefully and looking up from time to time.

'Which one?' Hasti asked, jostling Masti who nearly jumped on her.

'Keep quiet, you idiots, you'll spook them even before we start the hunt.'

'Okay, you guys, go and do your thing,' Phasti said. 'I'm off!' And she just disappeared, poof, she was just gone!

'How does she do that?' Masti asked plaintively. 'It's freaky!'

'She creeps me out, I tell you!' Hasti agreed. 'There's something weird about her!'

'Come on girls, let's go!' Zafraan, who as usual had been lying down regally, got to his feet.

The doe spotted the cubs from a long way off. She emitted a laconic snort, alerting the others.

'Beware! Beware! The morons are coming, the morons are coming!' she called, with mock panic in her voice. 'Come on girls, let's have some fun with them!' she grinned. She called out again, 'Come and get me babies, dinner is ready!'

Her friend looked around warily. 'Funny, their Mamma doesn't seem to be around!'

'These cubs have been here for a several days and no sign of their Mamma so far. They must be those cubs whose Mamma was shot recently. Everyone's been talking about them!'

'Then we're cool!'

'Babies, come on!' crooned the doe, stifling a giggle. She could see where the cubs were clearly—they left a trail of swaying grass as they moved through it, not to mention a flurry of moths and other insects that they disturbed. As they moved closer, she moved the same distance away so there was no chance of their coming close enough to catch her.

The doe's friend was also keeping an eye on the cubs. 'You know, I thought there were four cubs...' she said thoughtfully.

'Yeah, so?'

'There are only three in the grass!'

'The fourth one must have died... They've been motherless for three or four days after all.'

'I guess... *Watch out! Run!*' her friend shrieked suddenly and stamped her foot hard.

It was too late. A small tigress with blazing green eyes suddenly just erupted out of the grass from behind the doe and clamped her jaws around her neck before she knew what was what. She keeled over, kicking desperately, but the grip on her throat did not slacken. She struggled to her feet, kicking every which way, but the little tigress hung on grimly.

Little Phasti had sprung! While the other three had been distracting the doe, she had circled around her and had positioned herself perfectly for an ambush: the silly doe had been looking entirely in the wrong direction. And fortunately, there had been no breeze. Now the other three charged up. The poor doe gave them one look and her eyes rolled up as she fainted with shock. Then she was down, even as the rest of her herd thundered away across the grassy meadow.

'We did it!'

'Gimme five!'

'Awesome or what!'

'Come on, we better get it up to the cave! Hasti, Masti get a hold of her and pull; you too Phasti!'

Under the expert direction of Zafraan, shouting instructions, the three sisters tugged and pulled the doe's carcass up to their cave, panting and heaving.

'God, she's heavy!'

Hasti eyed Zafraan. 'Did you notice his lordship hasn't moved a muscle? He's just been shouting directions.'

'Typical! Mamma really spoiled him!'

The cubs feasted hugely that night; they really gorged themselves.

'That was so good!' Hasti purred, lying replete and doing her toilette daintily.

'Delicious!' Masti lay on her back, her paws in the air in a state of dizzy bliss. 'I can hardly move!'

'A kill never tasted better!' Zafraan looked at his kid sister. 'Baby, you were awesome,' he said as though bestowing a benediction on her.

'Yes,' the other two agreed. 'You were great!' They rolled their eyes at each other. 'Wow! Now bhai-jaan is calling her baby! Whaddya know!'

'Thanks,' Phasti said. And then added in a small voice, 'but I so wish Mamma had been here to see the hunt.'

※

'What are we hunting dinner tonight?' Hasti asked her siblings some nights later. The cubs had decided to stay on in the area where they had successfully brought down the doe. Their cave was well hidden, there was a stream and pools of water nearby, and there was dinner grazing on the meadow just ahead. Also, they were tired of being on the run.

'Let's stay here,' Masti had suggested. 'We're pretty far away from where Mamma was killed and it's nice here.'

'I feel like wild boar tonight,' Hasti said, licking her lips at the thought. 'Tender pork; we haven't had that for quite some time.'

Zafraan licked his lips and nodded. 'Yes, pork chops, that sounds good. And there's that noisy sounder that comes into the meadow every night.'

'We should go for a big one this time,' Masti said, 'those piglets are tasty but they're so small! Two bites and they're over!'

'Yeah, we should pick a real fatty, he won't be able to run very fast...'

'It'll be easy!'

Little Phasti looked a little doubtful. Considering she would be the one to make first contact with the boar, she'd have to bear the main impact and counter the defence reaction of the animal. A big boar could do a terrible amount of damage to a lightweight like her. But she couldn't let her siblings down, they had taken such good care of her ever since their Mamma had died. They depended on her for their meals.

'Okay,' she said softly, 'let's do it.'

They fanned out into the meadow that night and quickly picked their target.

'That one—she's really fat,' Zafraan said, indicating a huge sow which was moving about laboriously in the meadow, snuffling loudly. The rest of the sounder roamed around her, some mothers trying to control their broods, several young hirsute males and a couple of magnificent, mustachioed adults with deadly curved tusks, their tails up like the antennae on ministers' cars.

They had to be a little more careful while hunting wild boar. Hasti, Masti and Zafraan had to judge the distance they kept from their target precisely. They had to ensure that they were far enough from it not to panic it, but merely make it move away casually as they approached, towards the spot where Phasti would be lying in wait. At the same time, they had to make sure they didn't irritate it enough to prompt a charge, which would upset poor

Phasti's strategy completely.

The sow and a couple of other mothers with piglets spotted the three tiger cubs quite quickly. The mothers led their piglets away, but the sow was one stubborn thing. She eyed the cubs balefully and snorted. A couple of hirsute males with massive tusks watched her and the cubs from a little further away. And as usual little Phasti did her vanishing trick and slithered close...

She sprang and caught the sow completely by surprise. But it was tough trying to get her little jaws across that massive armored neck. She clung on, clawing at it desperately. Hasti, Masti and Zafraan charged, and then suddenly stopped dead in their tracks.

The two boars behind the female had put down their heads and were thundering towards them, grunting ferociously. The three cubs turned and fled.

The sow, which was immensely strong, flung off little Phasti as though flicking away a bluebottle. She turned and faced the dazed tiger cub who was scrabbling to her feet. The boar's little piggy eyes pulsed, red with rage.

'You little pipsqueak, now I'm going to trample you into the ground so hard you'll be one with the mud!' She pawed the ground like a Spanish bull and charged.

'Help!' Phasti yowled and turned to flee. Alas, she was back to being the clumsy little Phasti of old. She promptly tripped and went sprawling in the dust.

She could feel the ground tremble as the maddened sow thundered up to her like an enraged earthquake. She blinked. It was over. Mamma!

8

'You've scheduled the fight for twelve midnight?' Rana Shaan-Bahadur looked askance at Naradmunni. 'Are you nuts? Who the hell will be out at that time to take photographs or make a film?'

'It's all been arranged huzoor, do not worry!' Naradmunni wagged his tail ingratiatingly. 'The ramparts of the Sher-kila where you will fight are clearly visible from the veranda and garden of the Forest Rest House where Ayesha of the beautiful tresses is currently staying. Every night before going to bed she stands out in the veranda and brushes her hair 501 times. She'll hear you roar and will look up towards the fort... Imagine what she'll see! The full moon will be bathing the entire area in its lunatic silver light... She'll get fabulous footage. You'll be extra world famous again by dawn tomorrow, guaranteed money back! Besides these days, all major events are held at night lit by floodlights. You will have la luna to light you up!'

'You talk too much! Well... if you're sure!'

'Huzoor, we should set forth at around ten. We'll reach the venue by 11.30 p.m. and that'll give us enough time to scout the area and ensure that the devious Thug is not up to any tricks.'

'Very well.'

They set forth that night; Rana Shaan-Bahadur leading the way, furiously raking and spray marking trees as he went like any prize-fighter working himself up into the right testosterone-fuelled mood for the fight. Hah, he'd show that skinny wimp Thug a thing or two, daring to intrude into his territory! He'd be the champion of the world; his photos will make headline news once again! Those wretched genetically challenged cubs and their brainless mother would be long forgotten! How dare they steal his thunder! Furious, he attacked a venerable old sal tree, which protested indignantly, 'Hey cool it ustad, keep your aggro for the fight!'

Actually, what was annoying the big tiger was something he couldn't quite pinpoint but it kept niggling at the back of his mind like a sliver of sharp bone wedged between the teeth. Naradmunni followed warily in his wake.

A porcupine—an informer for the deadly Al-Seekh Kebab Atankvad Andolan—rattled its quills derisively as the great tiger passed by knowing it wouldn't dare attack it and risk injury while on the way to a title fight.

He scuttled off to report his findings. But already, word had got around, and a large number of animals were heading towards the fort to watch. This was going to be epic, the fight of the century! Herds of chital and sambar drifted towards the kila, and sounders of wild boar tried controlling their hyper-excited piglets as they took them out for this late-night outing. Even the langurs and macaques kept awake.

They were all glad of one thing: After this fight, they knew that one tiger would not be in a position to hunt them for some time to come. Hopefully, the two great tigers would kill each other and that would be two less tigers to worry about. Bets were being placed left, right and centre, and needless to add, Naradmunni as chief bookie stood to make a big killing (if you'd excuse the pun).

En route to Sher-kila, Shaan-Bahadur and Naradmunni arrived at the edge of the meadow in which the cubs had hunted. Naradmunni quickly ran up to Shaan-Bahadur.

'Huzoor, let me check if the coast is clear,' he said. 'Some of those sloth bears are completely psychotic and lie hidden, sleeping in the high grass till you're virtually on top of them. Then they stand up and download your intestines! Besides, I am sure that the porcupine we saw was a member of ASKAA—he might have tipped them off and they might be waiting to ambush you.' He looked martyred. 'If they kill me, you will know I died serving my master.'

'Are you drunk? How much mahua have you had tonight?' Shaan-Bahadur asked dangerously. 'Stop talking such rubbish!'

But Naradmunni merely shook his head sadly and scuttled off towards the meadow. He scrambled up a pile of rocks and surveyed the moonlit scene. There was a sounder of wild boar in the middle of the meadow looking intently at something in the grass. What was that? He followed their gaze. There were three trails of waving grass and jumping grasshoppers and agitated moths… something, well three somethings moving through the grass, leaving a clear trail. Naradmunni craned his neck. And then, as the grass parted he spotted the three tiger cubs clearly because they were really not attempting to conceal themselves. He recognized them in a flash.

The late Begum Raat-ki-Rani's orphaned cubs!

He gulped and then shook his head. The babies were obviously trying to hunt but the way they were going about it they wouldn't catch anything ever. The boars were quite nonchalant and didn't seem to be at all afraid. If the cubs continued to hunt this way they'd starve. And there was another more immediate problem:

What was he to tell their father, pacing about irritably nearby?

Shaan-Bahadur had vowed to kill the cubs. But maybe he wouldn't do so right now, not while on the way to a title fight. If he told Shaan-Bahadur that his cubs were in this meadow, he would definitely come back here after the fight to hunt them down and he would enjoy doing that. He would not risk leaving them alive so that Ayesha of the beautiful tresses could discover them again and make them more famous than he was, fight or no fight. Girls always went gaga over baby animals. Besides, as Shaan-Bahadur had derisively maintained, half the genes of the cubs (Raat-ki-Rani's share of course) were completely useless—look how she had allowed herself to be shot!

But he, Naradmunni of the fluttering heart and tender soul, couldn't do that. He couldn't condemn the cubs that way. They were doomed anyway. They were like a trio of idiot baby bulldozers in the grass; they would never make a kill. So why prompt the issue? If they could skirt the meadow, Shaan-Bahadur would never know that his cubs were there and they'd be safe from him.

He ran back to Shaan-Bahadur who was busy scratching up the trunk of a massive teak tree and squirting it like a fire hose.

'Huzoor, I've just heard from the grapevine that there is a bevy of sloth bears in that meadow and they're all in a foul temper and attacking everything that moves—apparently they ate some rotting fruit and have terrible tummy aches. Also, as I suspected, members of a suicidal ASKAA team are lying in wait like landmines. It would be better if we avoided the meadow. Of course, you could take them all down single-handed, but sire, you have a title fight up ahead and can't risk being injured. As your manager and trainer, I insist we go around the meadow and not through it.'

'Eh, what nonsense are you talking again?' the great tiger growled irritably. 'A bevy of bears, never heard of such a thing.' He looked towards the meadow and pricked his ears. 'I don't hear nor smell anything. We'll go through the meadow—it's much shorter.'

'Babies, I tried,' Naradmunni squeaked, 'but now it's out of my hands. Take care!'

'What are you mumbling now? Really, are you all right in the head?'

'Fine sir, I'm good.'

'Then come on.'

But Shaan-Bahadur too was a prudent tiger and leapt lithely up the pile of boulders from where Naradmunni had surveyed the meadow, to check for himself.

'What the...?' he growled, spotting the three tiger cubs in the grass at once. 'What the hell do they think they're doing?' A massive sow was eyeing the cubs and casually moving away from them—and towards him. Behind her two massive boars watched with upraised tails and smirks on their faces. If this had been any other night, Shaan-Bahadur would have made a quick kill and dined on pork...

'Those little fools! Do they think they can catch her like that? Where the hell is their mother? She's taught them damn all I must say!'

'Huzoor, she must be watching them.' Naradmunni swallowed the frog that had suddenly jumped into his throat, 'So I suggest we leave immediately. You know what these modern young tigress mothers are like… Completely hysterical and unpredictable! And you can't afford getting scratched, especially by a ballistic tiger-mom!'

'This is going to be so entertaining. Let's watch…it will relax me!' Shaan-Bahadur lay down regally, crossed his paws and stared at the cubs. 'That sow is suddenly going to charge them and play head butt with them all over the field!'

The breeze suddenly changed direction and blew up from the cubs straight across to where Shaan-Bahadur lay. He sniffed and stiffened. Heck, he knew that smell, it reminded him of something, someone…someone sweet and fragrant and almost forgotten. Someone who had purred at him like the engine of a Bentley and made him rumble deep down with unaccustomed pleasure.

Raat-ki-Rani! But Raat-ki-Rani was dead. And there was another smell too, a very familiar one—husky, musky and very macho and familiar. Naradmunni was watching him intently.

Realization dawned. Naradmunni nodded.

'Ji huzoor, they are yours and Raat-ki-Rani's cubs,' he said softly. 'Aren't they just *adorable?*'

Shaan-Bahadur swallowed. 'They're stupid,' he said shortly, getting to his feet. 'They're going to kill themselves. They're half full of their mother's dud genes after all.' He snorted. 'Saves me the trouble.'

But they were also half full of his magnificent genes and weren't those worth saving at all cost? Besides, the cubs were as Naradmunni had put it…what was that word he had used…?

And that irritation, chafing at the back of his mind, like the sliver of bone had suddenly become a full-blown ache of a type he had never experienced before. Like a huge tight knot that was stuck in his throat, preventing him from breathing properly. What on earth was happening to him?

'But of course it will save you the trouble, sir… So shall we be on our way?'

Just then, a fourth little cub with glittering jade eyes suddenly erupted out of the grass, and latched on to the massive sow's neck. She was facing him and for an instant Shaan-Bahadur looked into her eyes and gasped. It was like looking at a miniature reflection of himself which, of course, he did every day. Astounded, he watched as the three bulldozer cubs charged towards the sow, and then turned and fled as the two boars charged them. The sow flung the little cub off her and lowered her massive head and pawed the ground. She snorted and small clouds of smoke blew out from her flared nostrils.

'Oh no, angel face, no you don't!' Shaan-Bahadur growled deep in his throat. 'Not to my baby!'

Sprawled on the ground, her knees turned to water, little Phasti waited for the end. 'Mamma!' she whimpered. 'Mamma!'

There came a sudden flash of orange and black, like a flame leaping out of the grass. A blood-curdling snarl filled her ears and turned her tummy to liquid. There was a loud squeal followed by more snarling.

So this was it. This was what it was to be tossed and trampled into the dust by a wild boar. But wait a minute— was it? There was a huge striped creature sprawled over the sow, which was now kicking feebly and she, little Phasti, was okay. The legs stopped kicking. The creature released its grip and turned its massive head. Phasti stared mesmerized into blazing green eyes, just like her own.

'Papa?' she whispered. 'Are you Papa?'

He glared at her. 'You kids!' he growled. 'Just what the hell did you think you were doing?' Shaan-Bahadur shook his head in amazement; that huge tight knot inside him had suddenly come undone. His eyes softened and he walked towards her.

'Yo, baby,' he rumbled, licking her face. He looked around hastily. 'Now let's get the hell out of here before someone sees us.'

Phasti looked around puzzled. 'The others? Where've they gone?'

Indeed there was no sign of her siblings.

'Come on, let's go. We better get this fat pig under cover before those infernal hyenas smell her.'

Phasti suddenly arched her back and rubbed her face against that massive furry chin. 'I know where we can take it, Papa,' she said. 'And I know probably where the others are too... Follow me.'

🐾

In the cave, the other three were in a state of shock.

'We just had to run,' Hasti said defensively, pacing agitatedly up and down. 'Those guys would have ground us into the dust.'

'Yes,' agreed Masti, not sounding convinced at all. 'They were coming at us at 90 kmph!'

'We should have chosen another target,' Zafraan said heavily.

'How were we to know the fat woman had a couple of bouncers as back-up?' Masti asked plaintively.

'Do you think they've killed poor little Phasti?'

'What else? Did you see how their eyes glow red when they're angry...?'

But now it was Masti's eyes that had widened, as she looked towards the entrance of the cave.

'What's the matter?' Hasti asked. 'You look like you've seen a ghost...'

'Behind you...' Masti whispered.

Hasti and Zafraan turned around.

'Hi guys,' little Phasti chirped from the entrance. 'Papa's just brought us some dinner!'

And from a little distance away, craning his neck to get a peek into the cave, Naradmunni the jackal watched—and wept.

9

One hour after the scheduled start of the fight, Thug posed magnificently on the ramparts of the Sher-kila and proclaimed himself alpha male of all Sher-kila. That arrant coward, Rana Shaan-Bahadur had failed to appear; it was a walkover. The deer, wild boar, monkeys and other creatures which had gathered to witness the fight, grimaced. Thug sometimes just killed for the fun of it. The other tigers gloated, while the tigresses were surprised and well, a bit bitchy.

'What a coward!' Caligua posted.

'Yes, and now I'm going to have a go at Thug!' Atilla responded. 'Watch this space!'

'A no-show from Handsome Hunk! Imagine!' Resham scratched sarcastically.

'He chickened out! What do you know?' Razia sprayed. She was ecstatic. Thug was her partner. 'I'm First Tigress now!'

'Not for long sweetheart, if my Taimur has his way,'

Resham responded.

'Something terrible must have happened!' Only Lolita remained loyal.

By the following evening it had become quite clear. The mighty Rana Shaan-Bahadur had vanished! As had his slimy batman, Naradmunni the jackal, who had lost a fortune thanks to the fight fiasco. A number of furious animals who had bet against Shaan-Bahadur were on the lookout for him to collect their winnings.

In the cave above the meadow, the cubs delightedly roughhoused with their father, while Naradmunni daringly slunk away to gather information. He just had to put his ear to the ground and nose to a tree to become abreast of all the juicy happenings in the park. But the tidings he brought back to Shaan-Bahadur were not good.

'Huzoor, the vile Thug has proclaimed himself alpha male,' he submitted humbly. 'And the other foul felines are laughing.' He kept an eye on the cubs, who had taken to suddenly jumping on him and rolling him over.

Shaan-Bahadur nodded, looking bemused. He still couldn't understand it. He ought to have been in a towering rage; he ought to have wanted to tear Thug limb from limb; he should have been foaming at the mouth; instead he found himself gently batting around these clumsy tumbling cubs half-full of their mother's useless genes and was supremely happy doing so. Now *he'd* been purring like a Bentley! Was, god forbid, he going gaga and goo-goo?

'It's worse than you think,' he told Naradmunni. 'We have to leave the area. Sooner or later news will get around that we're here. And when it gets known that the great Rana Shaan-Bahadur gave up a fight in order to rescue and play with his cubs...' The great tiger shuddered. 'My name will be dung. I will never be able to show my face to any animal again.'

Naradmunni looked worried. 'So what are we going to do? We can't stay here, you are right, huzoor. Already the rumors are buzzing about where we are...'

'We leave tonight,' Shaan-Bahadur said. He spat. 'Imagine, I, Rana Shaan-Bahadur like a weasel on the run!'

Naradmunni looked stricken. Was the great tiger having second thoughts? Was he about to abandon his cubs?

'Huzoor, what to do? The babies need you!' he said quietly.

'I know. They have a lot to learn.'

'They were managing quite well; they'd developed a strategy to hunt together, but....'

'But that's not the tiger's traditional way. Lions may have joint families and hunt together, but we're proud individuals. We hunt alone! The little one is good, except that she needs to choose prey she can handle, but the other three—they have a long way to go before they'll be independent hunters.'

'So, um...where exactly do you have in mind, huzoor, if I may be so bold as to ask? We go outside the boundaries of the park?'

'No! We go to Taboo Valley!'

'What? Huzoor, you can't be serious! You can't take these delicate little things to Taboo Valley.' Naradmunni's eyes were wide with horror.

Rana Shaan-Bahadur's eyes glinted. 'We'll be safe there.'

'But...but...you know...what happened there... what the villagers did...'

'They've been moved out,' Shaan-Bahadur said. 'And there are no dead buffaloes there anymore...'

'But...but huzoor...they wiped out the vultures with their poison! And you know what kind of constitutions *vultures* have—they can digest anything—yet they died like flies! That hideous Diclo-Fenac couple barely escaped with their lives! You know it was decreed that no carnivore will hunt again in Taboo Valley, lest the same happens to them!' Naradmunni began sputtering. 'Huzoor, as it is there are so few tigers left—each cub is worth its weight in gold—you can't take these precious things there!'

'Will you stop yapping like a hysterical Pomeranian and listen? I studied the facts pertaining to the great holocaust. If you will recall, only vultures died. They got sick after eating those dead domestic buffaloes, which had been given some drug to make them give more milk, and which, when they died, were dumped outside the village where the vultures gorged on them.'

'Ninety-nine per cent died! Ninety-nine per cent, huzoor! What a kill ratio!'

'Yes, it was a wipeout! But only vultures died. As a precaution we decreed that no carnivore eat dead domestic buffaloes in the valley and then of course thanks to the general hysteria, it was deemed that all hunting in the valley be banned. Carnivores left the valley en masse.' Shaan-Bahadur's green eyes glinted. 'But the herbivores have stayed on there and multiplied; it's become a vegetarian paradise. They've probably already become lax and lazy in their ways because of the lack of predators. Easy meals! A great place to train those three clumsies to hunt! That's where we're going!'

'But...but...' As a consumer of carrion like the dreadful Diclo-Fenac, Naradmunni was perhaps correct in being worried.

'Besides, the problem was not confined to Taboo Valley. It's happened pretty much all over the country. And so far, only vultures have been affected!'

'So far huzoor, so far...Who knows what the morrow brings?'

'True, but we can't live in fear of that all the time. We leave at dusk!'

They set out at nightfall, heading due south, back past the rock-faces and cliffs where the cubs had been born and brought up by Raat-ki-Rani. Shaan-Bahadur led the way, followed by Zafraan, Hasti, Masti and little Phasti struggling at the end of the line to keep up. Naradmunni kept a special eye out for her, as he circled the straggling procession making encouraging noises.

'That's the way baby, be careful of that vine, it'll trip you up! Good, very good...that's the way!'

The cubs paused as they went past their old home and playground, gulping. Shaan-Bahadur stopped and looked back at them.

'What's the matter? Hurry up. We have to take cover at dawn!'

'Papa, this...this is where Mamma...'

'It's all right babies,' he rumbled in that deep baritone that made Phasti feel totally safe. 'I know. Remember it for all the happy times you had here.'

'Yes, Papa,' they chorused in small voices and scampered after him.

Three nights later, they were still on their way and the cubs were exhausted. They travelled at night, lying low during the daylight hours to avoid detection (which made Shaan-Bahadur extremely irritable). But he set a very brisk pace and was now getting impatient to reach.

'Come on, you lot, hurry up. The sooner we reach the better!' He looked back at his struggling brood as they followed him over the rough terrain, complaining plaintively.

'Papa, we're tired!'

'I'm hungry.'

'I'm thirsty!'

'Do we have to go to this godforsaken place?'

'What was wrong with the meadow?'

Only little Phasti gamely followed her father without complaint, tripping and stumbling like she always did, but keeping her mouth shut.

'Just pipe down and stop whining, will you?' their father growled, losing his patience and wondering what the hell had prompted him to take charge of his brood. He ought to have left them in the meadow. But then he looked into little Phasti's (easily his favourite) feisty green eyes and knew there was nothing else he could have done. She was struggling now as they clambered up the steep smooth rocks, slipping and sliding and landing on her tummy with a whump but never complaining. Suddenly she stumbled and rolled down several feet, landing flat on her tummy again, her breath whooshing out of her.

'And Phasti came tumbling after!' sang Hasti, as she and the others watched and giggled.

Shaan-Bahadur walked over and gently picked up the winded little tigress. 'Come on baby, let's go,' he growled.

'Papa spoils her…'

'She's his favourite…'

'We're like his step cubs!' Masti sniffed affronted. 'Like we're adopted!'

'I mean, what's his problem?' Hasti rolled her eyes. 'I mean, he was big dada tiger in the park and now we're fleeing like we're vermin or something.'

Zafraan, lying down regally cross-pawed as always, shrugged. 'I guess he has a point. He's this macho guy, the alpha male and all that, and is suddenly saddled with babies like you! I wouldn't like to be in his paws... The other tigers must be laughing at him.'

'You wouldn't know what the hell to do with babies either,' Phasti said indignantly. 'At least he's taken us under his wing.'

'Besides, you'll never be a macho guy!'

'Or have babies either.'

'And, it's such noble work!' Hasti added virtuously, 'there's nothing nobler than having babies and bringing up cubs, especially since there are so few of us left. I'm going to have lots of them.'

'Come on now, we're almost there!' Shaan-Bahadur encouraged his family on the fourth night. 'We should be there by dawn!'

Ahead of them loomed a solid rock wall, more formidable than any fortress.

'Papa, where do we go?' Hasti asked.

'There's a wall right in front of us!'

Naradmunni smiled. 'Babies, Taboo Valley is beyond the wall...'

'We...we have to climb up that?' Hasti paled.

'Papa, you can't be serious!'

The three older cubs just sat down astonished. The break enabled little Phasti to catch up with them.

'Are you coming or not? Now get off your butts and move!'

The big tiger began leaping up the rocks.

'Papa!'

'Wait for us!'

'Don't leave us!'

'Go! Leave us! Abandon us!'

'As if we care!'

Again, only little Phasti gamely tried leaping up the sheer rock-face as her father had so easily done. But for the cubs, it would clearly be impossible; it was just too high.

'That's the way, baby!' he growled as Phasti leapt up and fell back repeatedly. 'She has more guts than the three of you put together,' he called out to the others.

Grinning, he jumped down fluidly, picked Phasti up and leapt up again.

'Who's next?' he asked laconically, 'or do you lot want to stay here?'

One by one, he carried the cubs up the impossibly steep sections.

Tired and footsore, they scrambled up to the top of the ridge just as the sky in the east began to lighten.

'Take a good look,' Rana Shaan-Bahadur told them as they stopped for a breather. 'And welcome to your new home—Taboo Valley!'

It was in fact, a smaller version of the Sher-kila National Park: rugged ferocious cliff faces ringed around a forested valley, interspersed with grassy meadows. A broad stream ran through the middle of the valley into a blue lake studded with purple and yellow water lilies. One end of the lake had been dammed to form a water tank. Beyond the tank lay the ruins of the evacuated village. Houses and huts crumbled into rubble as the forest reclaimed them, bordering grasslands where once the villagers had grown their crops. Even from this distance, the cubs could see deer and antelope—sambar, chital and nilgai—grazing placidly in the grasslands, while wild boar rooted around the edges of the lake. A crested serpent eagle screamed as she flew overhead and snow-white egrets fished in the lake.

'Papa, I'm hungry! Hasti said, licking her lips at the sight of all that game.

'Me too!' Masti added.

'Umm, Papa, but how do we get down into the valley?' Zafraan asked, not daring to look down the sheer cliff face.

'We can jump!' Phasti said airily. 'We always land on our feet!'

The cubs rocked with laughter and Phasti smiled sheepishly.

'Yeah, yeah, okay, okay, I know...'

Naradmunni had been looking at the valley with apprehension. He had been expecting to see skeletons of animals and birds strewn everywhere, but the herbivores here seemed to be in excellent health and spirits. Perhaps Taboo Valley was no longer as dangerous as it had been made out to be.

'Come on, kids,' Shaan-Bahadur headed for a deep overhanging rock and to the cubs' consternation disappeared into it.

'It's the opening to a cave which leads to a long underground tunnel that runs alongside a stream,' Naradmunni explained. 'Unless you're a mountain goat it's the easiest way in and out of Taboo Valley. Now, after you, my dears...'

The tunnel was dark, steep and slippery (poor Phasti had a tough time), but at last they emerged into the open, a deep gully through which the stream ran, abutted by sheer rock-faces to which thorny bushes and scraggly trees clung tenaciously. They made their way to the edge of the gully, where the stream ended in a small waterfall and tumbled into the valley floor.

'Okay, you lot, sit and stay. I'll get us something to eat,' Shaan-Bahadur growled.

'But Papa, Mamma always took us hunting with her,'

Masti said, blinking her blue eyes. 'We were of invaluable assistance to her!'

'We have to learn,' Hasti giggled. 'Or Mamma said we'll be useless little prima donnas!'

'Papa, let the girls stay. I'll come with you,' Zafraan said, earning glares from his sisters.

Poor Phasti just lay down with her legs splayed out, enjoying the coolness of the rocks. She was beat.

'I told you, sit and stay! If little Phasti feels up to it, she can give you a lecture on stalking and how to approach prey without sounding like a JCB...'

'Sure Papa, I'd love to!' Phasti said, suddenly perky again.

'That's my baby!'

Hasti and Masti rolled their eyes. 'She has him round her little finger,' Hasti whispered to Masti.

'Did you know, some of the tigers in the famous Ranthambore National Park had started hunting in water?' Zafraan said, lying down and crossing his paws. 'I read that in a book.'

'Try that in Magar-Machch's pond and see what happens to you!' Masti retorted.

'Huzoor, some big, bristly sambar in the grassland just ahead,' Naradmunni reported. He'd been scouting ahead cautiously, alert for the terrible stench of death by foul medication. But his nose told him that Taboo Valley seemed to be an exceptionally healthy place with clean air and clear water and juicy prey. After the diclofenac holocaust, most of the herbivores, as well as rodents, monkeys and reptiles had stayed on happily because they had not been affected at all. To their huge delight, the great predators and scavengers had fled, and the villagers had been evacuated along with their dogs and livestock which ate up everything. For the wild herbivores, Taboo Valley had turned into a Garden of Eden.

Rana Shaan-Bahadur followed his batman out of the rocks and tested the wind. He could see the sambar up ahead, browsing, quite relaxed. He put his head down and began his stalk.

Far away in her Forest Rest House, Ayesha was distressed. Suddenly all the charismatic, photogenic tigers in the park had disappeared! First, the beautiful female with cubs had been killed by poachers and her cubs had vanished. Then that big show-off dude who she had made famous had stopped strutting his stuff from the ramparts of the fort and had disappeared too.

'He might have been killed in a fight!' one of the rangers told her.

'That guy was such a show-off he would have put an ad in the papers if he were to fight.'

'Sometimes these quarrels just flare up, like road rage…'

'Surely we would have heard them fighting or it would have been reported by the staff.'

'True. Ma'am, maybe you should just keep a good eye on the vultures. If there is a dead animal around, they're the first to find it.' He shrugged. 'There are so few of them left, maybe just six or seven, so keeping track of them shouldn't be difficult.'

'Thanks, I will!'

So that's what Ayesha did. She would drive up to a vantage point and scan the skies. Invariably, by around eleven in the morning (vultures are usually late risers) she'd spot the huge birds circling and wheeling high in the blue heavens. And once they'd start spiraling down, she'd drive towards the spot, hoping to come across a kill...or some clue as to the whereabouts of the missing tigers.

In Taboo Valley, the cubs and their father settled down, much to the consternation of the resident herbivores. To her delight, Shaan-Bahadur had put little Phasti in charge of giving the others hunting tuitions, while he himself (occasionally joined by his son and heir Zafraan) watched from the shade of a tree as she put them through their paces.

'Hasti, stop giggling!' Phasti hissed angrily, as her sister tried stalking a paddy bird. The bird croaked derisively and flew off. 'Can't you be serious for a second? Hunting is about life and death.'

'Cool it chick, Papa's always there...'

'And so are you!'

Masti was slightly better, and Zafraan, when he did bestir himself, managed quite well too, being keen to show off before his father.

Naradmunni would slink out of the valley from time to time into the main section of the park, to meet up with his missus and pick up the latest news and gossip. He returned one afternoon, looking quite vexed.

'Huzoor,' he said, 'you know those filthy hyenas who call themselves Gigglers?'

'No! I don't deal with scum!'

'Of course not, but apparently they're now looking for the cubs. And they've teamed up with those terrorist porcupines belonging to ASKAA who are determined to destroy all tigers in general and your goodself and the cubs in particular.'

'What?'

Naradmunni swallowed. 'Apparently huzoor, Missy Phasti bit off the tail of the leader of the Gigglers. They call him Dum-kutta now and the whole gang is furious and wants revenge.'

'They should know better than to come anywhere close to the cubs.'

'It gets worse, huzoor. ASKAA has sworn vengeance because apparently the cubs once tried to assassinate their commander by bouncing on the roof of his hideout in order to make it fall on top of him. He only escaped after a furious fight!' He paused. 'And you yourself have fearlessly hunted and killed and eaten several members of ASKAA.'

The cubs' jaws dropped. 'Papa, that horrible porcupine is lying!'

'We didn't try to kill him.'

'We only wanted to see what was inside the hole!'

'There was no fight.'

'Mamma got real mad at us!'

'But she did say you taught her how to eat porcupine!'

Naradmunni went up to the great tiger; it always made him a little nervous to get so close, but this was not meant for the innocent ears of the cubs.

'And huzoor,' he whispered, 'it is said that the luscious Lolita is extremely upset by your apparent disappearance; she's been caterwauling heartbrokenly every night from the ramparts of Sher-kila…'

'Let her. I told you she plays fast and loose!'

'Of course, sire!'

Indeed, while the other big daddy tigers in the park, Thug, Taimur and Caligua, had been pleased and secretly relieved by Shaan-Bahadur's apparent disappearance (an act of total cowardice of course), the tigresses were puzzled and upset. Like him or not, Rana Shaan-Bahadur was the finest, most handsome tiger they had ever set eyes upon and his absence was keenly felt.

'He must have got himself killed or shot!' Lolita sprayed sadly on her tree trunk message board. 'He actually ate at my table.'

'I think of him and my knees still fold up!' Resham admitted, suddenly nostalgic.

'Do you think he's done something silly because that idiot Raat-ki-Raani got herself killed?' Razia wondered. 'What a fool!'

The messages flew back and forth:

'I can't believe he chickened out of a fight.'

'Especially against that moron Thug.'

'He's not a moron.'

'Is too!'

'Is not and speak respectfully of him. He's boss tiger now! And I'm First Tigress, so mind your manners, madam!'

'He's not a patch on Shaan-Bahadur.'

'I miss him so much,' Lolita sighed. 'Just so much!'

'I wonder what happened to Raat-ki-Rani's cubs. They vanished too.'

'Must have starved by now!'

'Good riddance.'

Diclo and Fenac and their squadron too were on the lookout for the cubs. Every time they spotted a kill they would circle over it, hoping that they'd come across the cubs, either dead or alive. Preferably dead, because then they could boast that they had actually dined on tiger meat and their prestige (and power) in avian society would soar.

Dum-kutta the hyena was still livid. He'd noticed that even the other Gigglers had, ever since his 'accident', begun giggling one hell of a lot more than usual especially in his presence, even if it was just behind his back.

'I'm going to bite off the head of that cub, see if I don't!' he swore. 'Now, any rumour or news as to where they may be hiding, the miserable wretches?'

'No,' said his second-in-command, wagging his tail and giggling. 'But as you know, we've entered into an alliance with ASKAA to hunt them down collectively. They've sworn to stab out the eyes of the cubs and destroy all tigers.'

'Well get off your butts and find the cubs!' fumed Dum-kutta, licking his bum, which was still tender as a grilled tomato. 'Stop sitting there dribbling like idiots!'

'We attack all tigers but remember: Rana Shaan-Bahadur and those cubs are on the top of our hit list. Intelligence tells us that the cubs are in fact his, which makes it doubly important!' Col. 'Cuddles' Khujlimal rattled his quills ferociously. 'Shaan-Bahadur has killed and eaten several of our members and he'll teach his filthy progeny to do the same! We have to eliminate them.'

'Slow death to tigers! Slow death to tigers! Slow death to tigers!'

As one, the smelly members of ASKAA grunted and rattled their quills.

10

'Just listen to her!' Hasti muttered indignantly.

'Such a prissy missy!' Masti agreed.

'Lions have a much better system,' Zafraan averred, stretching languidly. 'The females do all the hunting and offer their kills to their lordship. That's how it ought to be!'

'Dream on, bhai-jaan, and don't butter up Phasti so you can swipe her kill!'

'Okay you kids, get off your butts!' Phasti's feisty green eyes glittered as she bustled up to her elder siblings. 'You're going solo today! No kill, no meal!'

'Sez who?' Masti asked dangerously.

'Papa!' Phasti blinked primly. 'So move it, babes! Okay, draw lots—who's the lucky one today?'

From the shade of an overhanging rock, Shaan-Bahadur watched proudly as his littlest one put the other three louts through their paces. She was enjoying herself to the hilt!

Zafraan yawned and got languidly to his feet.

'Watch me!' he told his sisters. 'And learn!'

Hasti nudged Masti. 'By the time he gets down to the grasslands, we'll be dead of starvation.'

'And boredom!'

'Yo bro, go get them!' Phasti said chirpily. 'Don't forget to check the wind direction or you'll spook them before you even get there.'

'Sure, sure kiddo, don't you worry!'

'God, is he insufferable or what!' Masti said, grimacing. 'And that silly Phasti just takes it!'

'Anyway, let's watch this; it ought to be fun!'

'Fun...in...slow...mo...tion!' Hasti intoned, dissolving into giggles.

Zafraan had slunk out from the shelter of the rocks and entered the golden grasslands. A troupe of langurs had foolishly come down from the trees and was frolicking about in the abandoned village, darting amongst the ruined huts and houses, pretending to be human beings. They lay in postures of abandonment along the walls and roofs or chased each other through the windows and doorways. Zafraan approached with caution, checking the wind direction every now and then and licked his lips. He loved langur. He crouched beside a hillock and studied the scene carefully.

Watching him, his sisters (except Phasti) were not impressed.

'He's going to be there all day!' Hasti giggled.

'Has he gone to sleep?'

'I don't know about him, but I'm about to.'

'Keep quiet you two!' Phasti hissed. 'Let him do his work!'

'Wake me up whenever…'

Zafraan had by now edged himself right next to the house closest to the border of the grassland. He'd noticed a pattern in the play of the monkeys. They would pick a house, race up to its roof, leap down, chasing each other and then race up again and repeat the process. When they got bored, they just went to the next house and did the same thing there. They were now two houses away from the one he was crouched next to… All he had to do was to wait—and not fall asleep of course.

He crouched down in the grass, his eyes on the shrieking monkeys. They were in high spirits, leaping and bounding. The guard monkey, sitting upon a rooftop, was himself distracted as he grabbed at the tails of his leaping compatriots. It had been a long time since any tiger or leopard had come this way, even though there had been rumors that a tiger and cubs had recently been seen in the valley. At any rate, tigers usually avoided places where humans had lived; the odour of all the evil deeds they had done lingered for a long time after they had left a place.

Zafraan's eyes were riveted to the cavorting langurs. With whoops they landed on the roof of the house just in front of him. Turn by turn, they leapt down into the dust and raced up again rather like children playing on a slide. For a second after they landed, they were stationary before they raced off. Zafraan wriggled to a place just ten feet from one such spot. His tail twitched with excitement. He hoped Phasti and the other idiots were watching him. This would be a lesson in ambush hunting—the tiger's way. Besides, langurs were not the easiest prey to catch; they measured pretty high up in the degree of difficulty.

A langur landed with a thump on all fours, exactly where Zafraan anticipated. With a growl, he leapt on it. It shrieked. And then Zafraan felt something land on the back of his neck, screaming with terror. The langur following the one he had pounced on had just leapt blindly off the roof straight onto the tiger cub's back.

The lordly Zafraan had a monkey on his back!

Panic-stricken, he reared up and the monkey he had pounced on wriggled free and fled. The one on his back jumped off and stared stupefied at the striped monster he had landed on. Then his eyes rolled up and he fainted with terror. About to flee, Zafraan saw it lying still in the dust. With a growl of triumph he pounced.

In the shelter of the rocks, Hasti and Masti rolled about in the dust, in hysterics. Even Shaan-Bahadur pursed his lips. Phasti smiled in delight as Zafraan walked over proudly with the langur in his mouth. He put it down and looked at his coach.

'Saw that? Got it in one!' he smirked. 'How many tiger cubs have been successful in their first solo attempt? Nothing to it, really! Hah!'

'Actually, bhai-jaan,' Hasti giggled, 'you didn't catch it—it caught you!'

'Then you grossed it out with your good looks and bad breath! Poor thing! What a way to go!'

Zafraan glared at his sisters. 'Ask for a tidbit and see what you get!' he snarled.

Phasti came up to him. 'Well done, bro!' she said. 'Granted you were lucky, but the fact remains you scored a direct hit on your first target and took advantage of the second one even if you were spooked at the time!'

Zafraan nodded deprecatingly. 'Wasn't spooked really, just pretending... Actually, I was hoping to kill two monkeys with one strike...'

'Yeah, yeah, sure!'

'Right, now you two others, it's your turn. We'll have to go to the other side of the valley, they must be on their guard here now.'

Hasti made a complete hash of her attempt. She picked a nilgai fawn and had managed to wriggle close enough undetected to launch an attack. Its mother was foolishly gossiping away with another doe and the fawn was lying down beside her. Hasti gathered herself for the leap, then suddenly thought of Zafraan with the monkey on his back. She giggled. The nilgai doe looked up in alarm, even as her fawn leapt to its feet and they were drumming away as Hasti stared at them in surprise.

'Hey, you, wait a minute!' she yowled. 'Get back here! Wait for me!'

Little Phasti was furious. 'You just don't concentrate, do you?' she raged. 'You have a mind like a…like a… feather in a storm. Well, Papa says you're to go hungry, maybe that will help you focus!'

'It's all his fault, Auntieji,' Hasti said, still bubbling with giggles. 'I thought of him just before leaping… The way that poor monkey landed on his back… The look on his face!' She dissolved into giggles again.

'Now you, Masti—listen up and listen good!' Phasti stalked around her elder sister. 'Imagine you have cubs back in your den. They're starving and have to be fed. If they don't eat, they die, savvy? It's your duty to bring them food. Now go and get some!'

'Really, Papa,' the earnest little tigress told her father later as they rested in the heat of the afternoon. 'Sometimes I despair of those two.'

'They'll be okay, baby,' he said. 'Don't you worry!'

But it was Rana Shaan-Bahadur who would have to do the worrying.

Wheeling in great circles two thousand feet above the park, a flicker of silver and puffs of dust rising from the ground from the southern-most section of the park caught Diclo's eye. He switched to telescopic mode and drifted in that direction.

But oh-oh, the activity was taking place in the middle of Taboo Valley. Even the airspace over Taboo Valley was restricted for vultures. He wheeled as close as he dared and focused.

'This is Delta, India, Cola, Lola, Ola to Funda, Eeta, Nina, Alpha, Cola, do you read me?' he radioed to Fenac. 'Fresh kill in Taboo Valley! Over!'

'Are you crazy? We don't go there! Over!'

'Natural kill, not domestic! One number langur monkey, being taken away by tiger cub...repeat tiger cub! Over!'

'Repeat, stay away from that airspace! Over!'

'Tiger cub now with three others and one adult male nearby! The fugitives have been located! Over!'

'Access denied! Repeat, access denied! That airspace is denied to you! Over!'

'Adult male positively identified as the missing Rana Shaan-Bahadur! Am flying over for a closer look; wish me luck! Over!'

'Are you mad? Over!'

'No dead buffaloes or traces thereof observed, over!'

Taking a deep breath, Diclo banked steeply and flew directly over Taboo Valley into restricted airspace, the wind whistling through his pinions. They had nearly died here, he and Fenac, and he would never forget the sight of sick and dying vultures clinging to the trees like so many Frankensteinian umbrellas. Only he, his partner and four or five others had survived the holocaust and now made up the entire squadron of the park. Fenac watched now, her heart in her mouth, as Diclo dropped height, his eyes peeled on the tiger family far below.

'Cannot believe visual! Male tiger is horsing around with cubs! Over!'

'What?' Fenac croaked, banking steeply. This, taboo or no taboo, she had to see for herself.

'Male tiger is playing, repeat playing with cubs! Frolicking, repeat frolicking with them! Disgusting! Over!'

'No need to shout, I'm right behind you. Am radioing squadron for backup! Over!'

'Seems quite safe... Oxygen levels normal, stench of death recorded between delicious and delectable, no trace of chemical or medicinal odour or disease! Over!'

'Then what are you waiting for, dodo? Commence descent...2,000-1,500-1,000-500-250...feet, landing gear down... On final approach... The vulture has landed!'

Folding her great wings, Fenac landed with a ghoulish hop, skip and jump, quickly followed by Diclo and then the rest of the Diclo-Fenac squadron. This they had to see, no matter what the risk.

A male tiger, a macho male tiger, playing and frolicking with his cubs! The great Rana Shaan-Bahadur was actually licking a little cub sitting under his chin, while three others attacked his flicking tail. The great tiger growled as the vultures landed and the cubs looked up. As one, they flew at the birds—no way that these filthy creatures were going to get a morsel of the langur Zafraan had hunted! The birds hopped away just out of reach.

'Tactical retreat, we've seen enough, over!' Diclo radioed, leaping and running clumsily as he took off. The others followed as the cubs and their father watched them go.

'I don't like this,' Naradmunni said darkly. 'It's a bad omen!'

From her vantage point on a hillock, Ayesha of the black tresses had kept her binoculars glued to her eyes. She followed the vultures' flight as they wheeled and then glided down into Taboo Valley and disappeared from view.

'They've found something behind those mountains!' she muttered. 'Better check it out.' She got into her Gypsy and roared off. An hour later she found herself at the foot of the sheer cliffs that guarded Taboo Valley. She parked under a tree and made sure her cameras were primed. Then she approached the rugged cliff faces on foot and dusted her hands on her dungarees. She had a Ph.D in Cliff-Climbing (otherwise you can't get a job with *National Geographic*), so these cliffs were chicken feed for her.

Pedalling behind furiously was Khoon-Pyaasa, following the dust thrown up by the Gypsy and its fresh tyre tracks in the path. He reached the parked vehicle an hour afterwards and dismounted. So, she had gone ahead on foot—but where? She was nowhere to be seen, and there were sheer mountains right in front!

There had been other (beady) eyes watching the vultures too. The Gigglers kept a close eye on the birds as they were excellent pointers to a kill. Normally the Gigglers preferred dining after dark when they could eat in peace but if the birds had found a promising enough kill, they would move in. This time, much to their surprise, the squadron landed on trees very close to where they were spending the time of day, resting.

'We have news!' Diclo said. 'We think you'd be interested in hearing...'

'Like what?' Dum-kutta looked up at the huge iron-coloured bird with distaste.

'You'll have to pay us for the information. First scavenging rights at any kill you appropriate for the next six months.'

Dum-kutta shrugged. 'That'll depend on the news!'

'It's to do with those tiger cubs that bit your tail off... Hahaha, that's just so funny!'

'What?' Dum-kutta cocked his head.

'We know where they are!'

'Nonsense! They're probably dead!'

'Surely you'll be interested in them dead…'

'Maybe!'

'So we know where they are. They're alive!'

'Rubbish!'

'Suit yourself. We'll inform ASKAA—they're after them too. And we'll tell them that we told you too and you didn't pass on the information to them. Then they'll come after you! Then you'll be Shri Pincushion Dum-kutta! Hahaha!'

The hyena eyed the birds balefully. 'All right, you have a deal! Hee-hee-hee!'

'Good! The cubs and their father are in Taboo Valley.'

'Hahahaha! You expect us to believe that?'

'Up to you,' Diclo ruffled the feathers on his shoulders. 'You can imagine what ASKAA will do to you when they realize you've been told and did not verify the information and chose to discard it. Especially since it's true…'

Dum-kutta glared at the birds. 'All right, we'll inform ASKAA.'

'Good luck.' Diclo prepared for takeoff. 'And don't try to conceal any kills from us, we have eyes in the sky. Hahahaha!'

'Very funny!'

Dum-kutta approached the headquarters of ASKAA with considerable trepidation. Members of ASKAA were highly unpredictable and usually impaled you first and asked questions later. The guard inside the mouth of the den backed out at a reckless 60 kmph, rattling his quills furiously. Dum-kutta yelped and danced clumsily out of range.

'Yikes! Watch it, Velveteen.'

'What do you want?'

'To talk to your boss, Col. Khujlimal. I have information.'

'Pertaining to what?'

'If I tell you, he'll kill me for that. Just call him.'

'Hmm...wait here.'

'Taboo Valley, eh?' Col. 'Cuddles' Khujlimal blinked his beady eyes and scratched his legion fleas. He nodded. 'Somehow I can believe that. Right, we leave tonight. Prepare to march. We take no prisoners. We spare no tiger we meet, inside the valley or outside. This is a declaration of war!'

At the headquarters of ASKAA an action plan was finalized.

'We follow them; we prick them off one by one. Once they're inside we block the tunnel exit so they can't escape and hit them hard!' Col. Khujlimal gloated, rattling his quills. 'Before you know it all the tigers here will be man-eaters and then be exterminated!'

No one quite knows how the other tigers in the park

heard the news about the fugitive tiger family, a little after Diclo-Fenac had been doing deal with the Gigglers. True, Naradmunni had left Taboo Valley on one of his forays into the main areas of the park at the time and, just might—*just* might, mind you—have let something inadvertently slip (leak, say the cynics) to his missus, who it was well known, could not keep anything to herself for more than twenty seconds tops. At any rate, the news, rumours, canards, call them what you like, in their various forms were being sprayed from pillar to post all over the park by its astounded, horrified and maliciously gleeful big cat population.

The great Rana Shaan-Bahadur was running a crèche for abandoned and orphaned tiger cubs in Taboo Valley!

The great Rana Shaan-Bahadur was doing what no macho tiger had ever done before—being a Mamma to his cubs!

The great Rana Shaan-Bahadur had broken an ancient tradition endangering tiger society the world over!

The great Rana Shaan-Bahadur was an official wimp and the laughing stock of Sher-kila National Park!

If the great Rana Shaan-Bahadur was the mother of the cubs, who was the father? Hahaha!

The tigers of the park stood united in their horror and condemnation:

Ths is unacceptable behaviour!

Hve 2 stop it!

Tradition cnot be trampled upon!
Hve 2 teach him a lesson!
Matter of gr8 shame!
Reputation of tigers at stake.
A dark day in the glorious hstry of *Panthera tigris*.
Our sentiments hv bin hurt!
Where's Jim Corbett when you really need him?
Kill the cubs! Kill Shaan-Bahadur!

The tigers and tigresses of the Sher-kila National Park now wanted to see for themselves exactly what was going on in Taboo Valley and then decide on the action to be taken to restore the lost glory and prestige of their species.

Outside the entrance to the cave and tunnel which led into Taboo Valley, Thug sprayed the rocks, outlining the strategy that would be adopted.

'First we set up observation posts around the perimeter of the valley and see what's going on. We must establish that Rana Shaan-Bahadur and his cubs are alive before we go down into the valley ourselves. We have to make sure there is no sign of the disease that wiped out those filthy vultures.'

'Affirmative,' sprayed the other tigers. 'Yes! We shall be happy to follow your lead.'

At intervals of an hour apiece, the great cats slipped into the cave and tunnel, wrinkling up their noses as they smelt the one that had gone just before them.

'That Caligua, he really stinks!' Razia growled to herself, 'hasn't bathed for at least a year! Makes me feel really queasy.'

Once they emerged on the high ledges that overlooked

the valley, the tigers spread around the perimeter, keeping as high up as possible amidst the rocks, so that they got a bird's eye view of the valley.

Razia found the best spot; it was high up and right ahead and below her was the water tank and meadow with its tall grass and the abandoned village beyond. She was the first to spot the fugitive tigers. They seemed healthy and fit. Even better, she had found a snug cave amidst these rocks. If it was safe here, this was the perfect place to have her cubs, which she knew were due quite soon.

'So this is Taboo Valley,' Thug muttered, still a bit nervous. He had stationed himself closest to the tunnel entrance so that if there was an emergency he could be the first to escape.

Down in Taboo Valley, Rana Shaan-Bahadur successfully brought down a large nilgai, on which he and his family feasted. Replete, they settled beneath a large sal tree, and the cubs began playing roughhouse with their father. He cuffed and batted them around, growling with mock ferocity, his green eyes glinting with pleasure. With pride, he noted that Phasti was turning out to be quite a bossy little thing, bullying her elder siblings into doing her bidding. She really was a talented huntress, and in a moment of rare candour he had to admit, better than he had been at her age. In fact, she reminded him a lot of Raat-ki-Rani. She had the same cunning and stealth that had made the tigress such a successful huntress. Maybe, just maybe, Raat-ki-Rani's genes were not all duds after all, even if she had let herself get shot. She had evidently passed on her splendid hunting genes to her little daughter. But yes, little Phasti had *his* jade green eyes.

'Yo baby,' he growled as she pounced on his head. 'You're just like your mother!'

Phasti purred like an electric motor.

Right then Naradmunni came tearing up, his tail between his legs, gibbering.

'Huzoor...they're here! They're coming after you! Flee! Run!'

'What are you yapping about again?'

'The other tigers! They're here. I smelt them all in the tunnel and nearly passed out! They're going to ambush us.'

'Just let them try!' Shaan-Bahadur's deadly claws slipped out and his voice rumbled malevolently. He rose to his feet.

'You lot, you stay here together,' he ordered the cubs. 'I need to check out a few things. Phasti's in charge!'

'Yes, Papa!'

'Why her?'

'It's always her!'

'You don't love us!'

'Or trust us!'

'Only her!'

Followed by a frantic Naradmunni, the great tiger set off along the stream towards the high cliffs that led to the tunnel entrance. He had not gone very far when he stopped, sniffed at a rock and grimaced. The message was clear and fresh.

My love!

Flee! They're here to kill you and your lovely cubs! And I...I will always love you!

Yours 4ever!
Lolita

'Run!' Naradmunni yelped, looking around fearfully.

'Thug!' Rana Shaan-Bahadur roared. 'Take your scum and get the hell out of here. This is my place!'

His roar echoed and reverberated around the great cliff walls. Every tiger heard it. Resham trembled—what a voice the fellow had. Lolita swallowed and choked back a sob. Razia felt her heart skip a beat. Caligua and Taimur looked down nervously at the stream below. Rana Shaan-Bahadur and that lackey cur of his was out there in the open, clearly challenging them.

As for Thug, he was having doubts too. He knew he had the advantage of height and numbers. If he and the others attacked, Shaan-Bahadur would stand no chance. Then why was Shaan-Bahadur challenging them openly? Obviously, Shaan-Bahadur had some powerful weapon or juju. As if to prove he was right, the sniveling jackal suddenly ran forward.

'Your lordships,' he yelped, looking up at the great cliffs. 'Your lordships, his exalted highness Rana Shaan-Bahadur has just dined on *buffalo*! A medicated buffalo! An infected buffalo!'

Everyone knew what dead medicated buffaloes had done to the vultures... This was Taboo Valley, after all.

Thug was horrified and his first instinct was to run for it. But to flee now would be to lose face—and he would be challenged by those other two, Caligua and Taimur who were just waiting for a chance to grab power. Thug backed away, snarling.

'Then we stay here and watch him and his cubs die!' he snarled. 'In the same horrible way that the vultures had died! I shall enjoy that!'

'Why the hell did you say that?' Rana Shaan-Bahadur snarled at poor Naradmunni, swiping at him with a paw. 'As if I were diseased!'

The jackal darted away. 'Huzoor, think of the cubs! If anything happens to you, who will look after them? They've been orphaned once, isn't that enough?'

Shaan-Bahadur rumbled deep in his throat as he thought of them: his beloved Phasti, such a talented huntress whom he still had to teach how to hunt porcupine. The other two happy-go-lucky ones, Hasti and Masti who somehow bumbled along; and then Zafraan his regal son, who one day would take over his territory... He backed away, rumbling angrily.

'Let any of them put one paw down here and see what happens!'

So the tigers of Sher-kila settled down to watch, waiting for the great tiger Rana Shaan-Bahadur and his cubs to sicken and die of the same foul disease that had killed off the vultures. And Lolita's tender heart fluttered just a little bit. Dare she hope?

It appeared that she could. Because far from showing signs of sickness, Rana Shaan-Bahadur and his family seemed to be thriving in Taboo Valley. The tigers of Sher-kila watched as the great tiger hunted nilgai and chital and sambar for his family; they watched him teach one of his cubs advanced hunting techniques, they watched the little one boss around her siblings and they watched the male cub, lying regally in the sun, with his paws crossed. They watched the way Rana Shaan-Bahadur played with and disciplined and fussed over his cubs; they knew the little green-eyed one was his favourite.

What they saw infuriated them. Razia and Resham were bitter with scorn.

'Look at him! He hasn't a clue how to bring up those cubs!'

'He's spoiling them sick!'

'They need to be spanked.'

'He needs to be banned from seeing them!'

'They're going to grow up to be rogues and vandals—man-eaters even!'

'Give us a bad name!'

But Resham and Razia didn't quite look each other in the eye when they made these accusations against Shaan-Bahadur. Lolita wisely kept her counsel because she ached to join the tiger family in the valley and mother the cubs—no matter that they weren't hers.

The tigers of course were outraged.

'What the hell does he think he is?' Thug ranted.

'He should have eaten those little monsters.'

'Raising cubs is a tigress's work. Period!'

'He's dishonoured us!'

'We need to kill him and his brood.'

'A killing to restore our honour!'

But like the tigresses, Caligua and Taimur looked shiftily away from each other as they raved and ranted because neither or them so far had the courage to actually get down into the valley and attack Shaan-Bahadur on what was now clearly his territory. Thug too was clearly uncomfortable and kept muttering about launching a 'three-pronged' attack when 'the time was ripe'.

Down in the valley, Rana Shaan-Bahadur continued coaching his cubs, as though everything was normal. It was poor Naradmunni who remained anxious, forever glancing towards the forbidding cliff walls where he knew the tigers lay waiting, biding their time. Before long, they would call his bluff and then there'd be no stopping a terrible bloodbath. He'd spotted the Diclo-Fenac squadron patiently circling above the valley and once or twice, thought he had heard the ghastly liquid laughter of the Gigglers. If the scavengers were already gathering, it was not a good omen.

And then, one morning, near the stream at the base of the rocks, he saw something that made his blood run cold.

Lying in a cleft between two rocks was a porcupine quill.

The dreaded Al-Seekh-Kebab Atankvad Andolan had caught up with them and had left its calling card.

Naradmunni carried the quill in his mouth to Rana Shaan-Bahadur.

'Huzoor, they're here!' he said, dropping it at his feet and trembling. 'ASKAA is here! We have to move out!'

'What?' Rana Shaan-Bahadur eyed the quill with interest. 'Good,' he went on, 'I'm glad they're here. Now I can teach little Phasti how to hunt porcupine, she's been dying to learn.'

Indeed, a suicide squad from ASKAA led by the terrifying one-eyed Col. 'Cuddles' Khujlimal had already slipped into Taboo Valley via an ancient secret tunnel excavated by rodents of yore.

'We terrify them first!' Khujlimal grunted as he deliberately dropped a quill amidst the rocks where Naradmunni later found it. 'Let them know we are here and tremble!'

'Boss, there are other tigers here too,' Major Khujahomujhe reported after returning from a recce. 'They're keeping to the ridges on the rock-face, but sooner or later they will have to come down to hunt.'

'It's open season, Major. We spare no one, but that tiger family down there is our top priority!'

'Yes, boss.'

'Major Khujahomujhe, you will accompany a party of three into the valley and sneak up to the tigers there early tomorrow morning. You stab them while they sleep. Just reverse into them at top speed and get the hell out of there. Embed as many quills as possible. That'll teach them to launch an unprovoked attack on my headquarters.'

'Yes, sir!'

Col. Khujlimal took a deep breath. 'You will be led by Lieutenant Col. Kabab-me-Haddi who has been promoted to this rank and suitably briefed. Is that clear?'

Major Khujahomujhe took a deep breath.

'Yes, sir!' he said, ever the obedient soldier, but with a sinking feeling in the pit of his stomach. He didn't like the fact that he had been superseded.

Lieutenant Col. Kabab-me-Haddi, alias 'Chuboo-Chuboo', the Col.'s younger brother, was rumored to have been bitten by a partially rabid bat when he was young. He was rather like that little girl with a curl in the middle of her forehead—when he was good (well, not good, just normal) he was very, very cowardly and when he was bad, he was rabid. It was always a huge risk putting him in charge of an expedition or mission. But, the Col. thought the time had come to blood the young Lieutenant Col.; time he proved his mettle.

The suicide squad set off before dawn the next morning. Rana Shaan-Bahadur and his family had taken over some of the less ruined houses in the village and slept here; it was quiet and comfortable. Naradmunni curled up at the doorway of the house, one ear flicking, an eye flickering, in case Shaan-Bahadur required anything. In any case, he had not been sleeping too well ever since he had found that porcupine quill. That morning, he awoke very early and trotted off into the meadow adjoining the village to do his morning ablutions, looking around warily all the while. Threading their way through the meadow, the suicide squad grunted and snorted, working themselves up into a rage. Ah, revenge was at hand and it would be so sweet! From his position, Naradmunni spotted them—four ferociously spiky monsters, punks from hell, trotting in single file at a good pace, along one of the narrow paths in the meadow and heading for the village.

He slithered his way out of the meadow in the way only a jackal could and raced off at top speed.

'Huzoor! Huzoor!' he whispered loudly, hoping that Rana Shaan-Bahadur would not be so startled as to leap awake and kill him.

'Hey Munni, what's up bro?' Hasti opened one sleepy eye.

'You look like you've got a flea up your bottom,' Masti giggled, opening another eye.

'Can't you let a fellow sleep in peace?' Zafraan protested.

'Is there a problem, uncle?' Phasti inquired, instantly alert.

'No, yes, big problem…wake your father right now!'

'Papa, wake up, Munni's got a flea in his bottom!' Hasti giggled.

Rana Shaan-Bahadur opened his eyes and yawned, displaying those fearsome canines.

'What is it?' he growled irritably. 'Do you know the time?'

'Huzoor, a squad hit from AKSAA is way on the here!' Naradmunni yelped, getting hopelessly mixed up. The cubs were beginning to giggle. 'I mean, a hit squad from ASKAA is on the way here. I saw them in the meadow.'

'Oh, is that so?' The green eyes glinted. Rana Shaan-Bahadur yawned again, stretched and got to his feet. 'So let us give them the reception they deserve.' He glanced at the cubs. 'You kids, you stay at the back of the house on the charpoys, no matter what. Phasti, baby, you watch me carefully…'

'Okay, Papa!'

There was only one doorway to the house through

which the suicide squad could enter. The stout wooden door still hung grimly to its hinges, though the door swung open and shut seemingly at will. It was nearly shut now, but the tigers knew that a nudge from their paws could swing it open. (The cubs had a lot of fun batting it open and shut.)

'Right, Naradmunni, get up to that window overlooking the door. Tell me when they're at the door…'

'Ji huzoor!' poor Naradmunni agreed, wishing they could all just flee. This was not going to be pretty. Porcupines were diabolical and members of ASKAA were reputed to have poison-tipped quills. 'But will the cubs be safe?' he asked.

'They'll be fine!' Shaan-Bahadur did a few dozen effortless crunches and crouched down. 'Now go!'

The hit squad had entered the village and was trotting down what had been the main road through it. Some houses still had precariously hinged doors, some didn't.

The mode of attack they used was simple. The porcupines would barge in single file headfirst, spot the enemy and do a swift handbrake turn and reverse into them at top speed and then shoot off.

'Right, here we go!' Major Khujahomujhe snapped as they stopped outside the first doorway. It stood open. He charged through, followed by the others, with Lieutenant Col. Kabab-me-Haddi bringing up the rear—and skidded to a halt. The house was empty.

'Clear! Take the next one!'

From a window just above the front door, Naradmunni watched in horror as the suicide squad entered one house after the other, barging in, doing stylish handbrake turns, barking out 'clear!' and then trotting out. They were approaching swiftly.

And then, they were outside the door of the house where Shaan-Bahadar and his family were waiting. Naradmunni looked down.

'Huzoor, they're here!' he whispered. The cubs' eyes widened as they lay in a row on the sagging charpoys and watched. They could hear the scuffling and snuffling of the hit team as they regrouped outside the door. Rana Shaan-Bahadur crouched on his haunches, his tail flicking. Naradmunni looked down and nodded again.

'They're just outside the door,' he mouthed silently.

With a roar that could give you an instant enema, (and poor Naradmunni squirted his tail) Rana Shaan-Bahadur leapt at the door and flattened it over the hit team.

Two members of the squad were horribly squashed and impaled by their own spines. Lieutenant Col. Kabab-me-Haddi, at the rear, turned around and fled gibbering with terror, shedding quills as he fled. Major Khujahomujhe received a glancing blow to the head as the door crashed down with the psychopathic tiger on top of it. Stunned, he reeled drunkenly and then saw the maddened green eyes of the tiger staring at him. With a deft flick of a single claw, the tiger flipped him over on his back...

'Come after my babies, will you?' he snarled. They were the last words Major Khujahomujhe ever heard.

'Awwwesome!

'Gimme five!'

'Way to go, way to go!'

'Papa-Papa-Papa!'

'You're the greatest!'

The cubs were ecstatic.

'Wait!' the great tiger growled. He leapt again on the door under which the two crack members of ASKAA had now indeed inadvertently committed suicide. 'Let me make sure this vermin is dead!'

He dragged the heavy door into the street and flipped it over. Impaled upside down in the stout wood by their own quills, the two members of the hit squad were as dead as they could be. Beside them in the dust, lay their leader Major Khujahomujhe, whose fleas were already evacuating at full speed.

'Breakfast is served, kids!' Rana Shaan Bahadur grinned. 'Now be very careful how you eat these fellows.'

Lieutenant Col. Kabab-me-Haddi fled back to his brother's hideout.

'Cuddles! I have terrible news!'

'What? And kindly address me by my proper name and rank! And where are the others?'

'Dead! Martyred! That crazy tiger killed them all with a single blow!'

'What?' Col. Khujlimal rattled his quills ferociously.

'We should leave this place right away! It is evil. It is not called Taboo Valley for nothing.'

'Stop whimpering!'

But now, even Col. Khujlimal was rattled. A crack hit team of fanatic porcupines had been decimated. The enemy had received not one quill. They had reduced his brother to a gibbering idiot! Perhaps it was time to pull out and rethink the strategy. He ground his teeth in rage and raced about in a fury, even as Kabab-me-Haddi trembled.

'I'll kill them, I'll kill them all, the infidels! They must die, they must die!'

He heard a growl and looked up. A tigress was standing in front of him, looking alarmed and angry. She growled again baring her teeth. Col. Khujlimal lost his head. He spun around and reversed full tilt towards the snarling animal. She leapt out of the way with a yowl and turned and fled.

'Take that! Flee! Coward! Long live ASKAA!' the mad porcupine screamed.

Razia raced back to her cave and lay down. Then she

began licking her paw and chest, moaning softly.

Embedded in them were a cluster of porcupine quills. ASKAA had finally drawn blood.

12

Thug paced about the rocks and ravines restlessly. He knew Caligua and Taimur were watching him, waiting for the slightest sign of weakness. Somehow, he had to attack the formidable Shaan-Bahadur and accomplish the mission that had brought them to this godforsaken place. It had brought all Shaan-Bahadur's enemies to this place he thought sourly—not only members of ASKAA, but also those ghastly hyenas who called themselves the Gigglers.

The Gigglers had indeed at last arrived, midst much nervous giggling. They knew a major killing was to take place and they wanted to be at hand. After dining on poor Raat-ki-Rani they had developed a taste for tiger meat. In spite of his bitten-off tail, Dum-kutta believed that ever since that memorable meal, he'd become a more macho hyena, one with the heart of a tiger. But the hyenas were wary of eating carrion in Taboo Valley and wished ASKAA and the other tigers would get on with the job of killing the fugitive family.

'What's with them—behaving like bureaucrats?' Dum-kutta muttered.

'They have a problem, sir. They're scared of the tiger.'

'Maybe they should join forces…' Dum-kutta muttered thoughtfully. 'I have an idea. I think I need to have another meeting with that ghastly Khujlimal. Arrange it, boy!'

'So here's the thing,' Dum-kutta told Col. Khujlimal a while later. 'Here's what you need to do…'

The Colonel heard him out, his single bloodshot eye widening. 'Do you seriously think this will work? The tigers may not be agreeable…'

'They will be!' Dum-kutta giggled. 'They want that tiger and his cubs dead more than anything, but they're scared. With this plan it will look as if you'll be taking the major risk. They'll only have to attack when he's already down and out… Once the cubs are dead, the fellow will just capitulate without a fight. Even I could kill him then!'

'Maybe you should then,' the porcupine said sourly.

'But don't you see—the risk for yourself and ASKAA is also minimal.'

Col. Khujlimal thought for a bit. 'Very well, now how do we make contact with the tigers without freaking them out? Such a deal has never been done before!'

'No problem. We'll broker that deal. We'll fix up the meeting for you.'

'What's your price?'

'Feeding rights to the cub kills! All four of them...'

'Agreed!' Col. Khujlimal eyed the hyena with disgust. 'You should try going vegetarian you know, it might improve your personality.'

'Hahaha for LOL!'

And so a historic meeting was held between Col. Khujlimal and Thug, with Dum-kutta acting as mediator and outlining his diabolical plan.

'You see your lordship, neither you nor the other noble tigers of the park will be at the slightest risk,' Dum-kutta gushed. 'No one need get the slightest scratch! Once ASKAA—that magnificent fighting force—takes out the cubs, the father will capitulate. Then you attack him, with ASKAA providing backup if necessary. Honour will be restored.'

'And what does ASKAA get out of this deal?'

Col. Khujlimal rattled his quills. 'The pleasure of killing those cubs slowly and painfully! They dared desecrate my hideout in the park by jumping—jumping mind you—on its roof while I was meditating and doing yoga and then attacking me like I was some sort of darpoke hyena—no offence to you, of course!'

'Haha, none taken,' said Dum-kutta, baring his teeth in a grin.

'Besides, their father has hunted and martyred several of ASKAA's fighters, including three just recently! Their deaths have to be avenged!'

'Certainly!'

'We will need details of layout, access, possible killing angles, risk of collateral damage...'

'Don't worry,' Dum-kutta said. 'I'll have all the info for you.'

Thug came away from the meeting quite pleased with himself. He sprayed the news of the meeting and the developments on the rocks—there was going to be a joint operation with ASKAA to eliminate Rana Shaan-Bahadur and his family. The details of the plan would be revealed on a 'need-to-know' basis.

The replies were encouraging. Caligua and Taimur were enthusiastic, as was Resham. Only Lolita was privately anguished and opted out. Surprisingly, there was no response from Razia. The tigers were not unduly worried.

'She was very near her time,' Resham sprayed. 'She's probably found a cave and will have her cubs there.'

'Best stay away, then,' Thug responded. 'I don't want her disturbed at such a time.'

'You'll get your head bitten off if you do!' Resham responded tartly.

And poor Lolita could only nurse her aching heart...

Col. Khujlimal too was quite satisfied. Once Rana Shaan-Bahadur was neutralized, the other tigers would relax and lower their guard... They would want to celebrate their triumph. That's when...

His brother, Lieutenant. Col. Kebab-me-Haddi was delighted with the plan. 'Can I lead one of the raiding teams?' he begged. 'I have to avenge Major Khujahomujhe's martyrdom!'

'You will be leading one of the teams. And I'll be leading the other!'

'When do we attack?'

'On the night of the next full moon,' Col. Khujlimal decided. 'That stupid jackal that hangs around with the tigers will probably spend the night howling at the moon and won't warn them...'

'Perfect! Oh Cuddles, I'm so excited!'

'*Don't* call me Cuddles, okay?'

'Sorry, Snuggles... Hee-hee...'

'And stay away from those wretched hyenas or you'll turn into one!'

High up in the sky, the Diclo-Fenac squadron watched over Taboo Valley and brought news to the Gigglers (they were promised exclusive leftover rights to the cubs by the Gigglers). They had been recruited by the hyenas to spy on the tiger family and report details of where they hung out and the hours they kept. One morning, not much later, they landed on some of the great rocks that formed part of the ridges of Taboo Valley, close to where the Gigglers were camping.

'We have news!' Diclo said laconically. 'The tiger family has moved.'

'Moved? What do you mean?'

'They've upgraded,' Fenac added.

'But moved where?' Dum-kutta was concerned.

'They've moved to the headman's house. You know, the one that is directly opposite the village temple on that small hillock?'

'Will it be easy to attack?'

'Depends…the house is built around a courtyard. There's one entrance. The doorways to the rooms on three sides also open into the courtyard. A mud wall separates the house from the streets outside. The cubs vanish into the rooms to rest and play in the courtyard with their father. They even dragged a kill through the doorway once and ate it there. They sleep in the rooms too. Their father prefers remaining in the courtyard. The jackal sleeps at the entrance.'

'How could an animal get inside without attracting the attention of the tiger or jackal?'

'There are two ways—either via the roof of the house, or tunneling under the wall and thereby getting directly into the rooms. I would recommend the latter, the roof is partly thatched and partially tiled, and doesn't seem too secure.'

'That's okay!' Dum-kutta was relieved. The ASKAA

hit team would have no problem tunneling beneath the boundary wall and straight into the rooms. It would be rather like a prison escape, though in the opposite direction. He lurched off to update Col. Khujlimal of the latest developments.

Indeed, Shaan-Bahadur and the cubs had moved. After the first abortive attack, Shaan-Bahadur decided they needed a somewhat safer residence. The village ex-headman's house was a much better bet. For one, the doorway was open, so you could immediately spot anyone outside in the street. Secondly, there was the courtyard, which gave one some fighting space in case there was an attack. Thirdly, the headman had left behind a number of sagging charpoys and gaddas, which the cubs loved lounging on. Directly opposite the house, across the mud-tamped street, on a small hillock was a neat little temple (once blinding white), in a small courtyard. Huge peepul trees grew on either side and were now beginning to spread their roots over the temple building itself.

Shaan-Bahadur was relaxing in the courtyard one sunny afternoon, thinking about the night's hunting (wild boar or chital?) when Naradmunni came running up in a lather of excitement.

'Huzoor...huzoor...'

'Munni's got another flea in his bottom!' Hasti sang as Masti joined in. Phasti just raised her eyebrows. Would her sisters just never grow up? Zafraan of course just sneered. His sisters were beyond help.

'What is it?'

'Huzoor, you remember that beautiful photographer with the long black tresses from the *National Geographic*? The one that made you world famous? The dhimchack chick?'

'What about her?' Guiltily, Shaan-Bahadur also remembered that he'd been jealous when the girl had gone and made Raat-ki-Rani and the cubs famous too.

'She's templing in the putting up door next!' Poor Naradmunni had tangled himself up like noodles on a fork again. 'I mean, she's putting up in the temple next door!'

'I see…'

'We're going to be world famous again. She has all her cameras and things; so wonderful, no, huzoor?' He swallowed. 'Such a pity begumji is not here…'

Shaan-Bahadur sighed. 'That can't be helped, I suppose.'

He got to his feet. 'How long has she been there? I didn't smell anyone there when I went for my morning stalk.'

'I think she just got here. She was settling down.'

'Papa, are we going to be famous?'

'Will we be going viral?'

Zafraan lay down and crossed his paws, clearly posing. Hasti and Masti pounced on him at once. Little Phasti shook her head in exasperation and went and lay down between her father's shaggy paws, her forehead rubbing against his furry chin.

And up in the temple tower, Ayesha of the long black tresses, crouched down behind her cameras, her face ecstatic, tears running down her fair cheeks.

There was no doubt in her mind. These were the cubs whose mother had been so cruelly shot by poachers. And now, now the little darlings were being looked after by their father—that very same magnificent tiger she had first photographed at the waterhole (with the poachers) and later, posing like some playboy dude on the ramparts of the Sher-kila. What a story this would make! It was too touching for words. It would be worth the trouble she had been put through in the last several days when she had searched for the tigers in Taboo Valley.

Firstly, for a photographer, the valley had been grossly distracting with its scenic vistas and teeming wildlife. She had at last come across pugmarks along the stream and then, tired of sleeping rough in some of the caves in the cliff faces (which could be very dangerous if a bear or leopard turned up), had moved into the village. She had been lucky that Shaan-Bahadur and his family had not got wind of her arrival because she moved as quietly as a tigress herself, and had been downwind of the tigers when she had arrived at the village. She'd decided to set up camp in the temple and then, to her total disbelief had discovered that her nearest neighbours were the very same tigers she had been seeking out so desperately.

But alas, she had not been the only human being to have entered Taboo Valley...

Scratched, bruised and bloody, Khoon-Pyaasa too had scaled the massive cliffs guarding Taboo Valley and looked down into the valley. He caught a glimpse or two of the tigers Thug and Caligua as they moved around the ridges and knew that this could be a happy hunting ground for him. And then, he had spotted the photographer girl. She was picking her way along the bottom of the valley beside a stream. He scrabbled down as quietly as he could and tracked and stalked her. He watched her as she camped out in caves and then followed her as she finally made her way to the village. He nodded, perfectly satisfied. Now he had her trapped. Then, just outside the village, he spotted the pugmarks of Shaan-Bahadur and the cubs in the dusty street that led into the village.

It was only a matter of time before he discovered the tigers' hideout. He eyed the roof of the headman's house and reckoned it was high enough to be safe from a leaping tiger. Best of all, he could sprawl on the roof like a proper assassin, look down into the courtyard, take his shots at the tigers, and then simply raise his gun and kill the girl too as she stared at the carnage in shock from across the road. A few minutes of good—and enjoyable—shooting is all it would take. But first, he would have to get on to the roof without being detected by the tigers...

13

'Come on kids, we're going hunting!'

'Yay!'

'Papa, may Hasti and I stay behind? We're tired. You can take Zafraan and Phasti.'

'Actually, I'd like to finish my book,' Zafraan said. 'This guy Kenneth Anderson is such a scream!'

'Move it! Hasti and Masti, this is going to be your hunt. You fail, we all starve tonight.'

'Papa, don't be so mean.'

'This is emotional blackmail!'

'Move your little butts before I smack them!'

'Okay, okay, only kidding,' Hasti giggled, enjoying her father's irritation. 'Chill, man!'

'Babies, there are some juicy tender chital on the other side of the lake. They look really inexperienced and stupid.' Naradmunni ran up and down excitedly wagging his tail. 'Should be easy for you girls!'

'Thanks, Munni!'

'Papa, when can we hunt porcupine again?' Phasti asked. 'They were absolutely delicious!' Her sisters made a face.

'Look who's showing off again!'

'Little Prissy Missy wants porcupine!'

'By and by, baby—those fellows I killed must have friends nearby. We'll get them at some point.'

'Great, Papa. Yes, one of them ran away!'

They entered the grassy meadow, crouching low and blending perfectly with the golden grass. 'Okay Phasti, you direct them!'

'Sure, Papa. Right, Masti and Hasti, it's going to be separate targets for you. See that one near that crooked tree—he's yours, Masti. Hasti, you take that fellow near the water. He's going to drink soon…'

'But he's got horns!'

'Of course he has. He's a stag.'

Zafraan shook his head. 'This is not going to work…'

'Shut up, Zafraan. Okay, now you two, crawl as close to them as you can without being seen. You'll have to be on red alert. Hasti, if you spring first, Masti's kill will bolt, so she must be ready for that. The same holds true the other way round. It's rather like what Mamma taught us, remember? One, two, three, four…ten!'

'Very clever!'

'Stop fussing and go!'

Rana Shaan-Bahadur just lay down and watched.

Zafraan sat beside him, his usual snooty expression on his face. Naradmunni came trotting up.

'Huzoor, that dhimchak chick from NG has followed us. I think she wants to photograph the hunt.'

'Stop calling her a dhimchak chick—that's disrespectful. Let her take her pictures. I just hope the girls don't make fools of themselves. If they do, we'll have to eat her and her camera!'

'They'll be fine, huzoor.'

'Hah, I'm going to enjoy this!'

Hasti and Masti set forth after the targets chosen for them. Keeping low in the golden grass, they stalked their prey, checking the wind direction every now and then. To their immense surprise, both of them suddenly found that they were actually enjoying themselves. Suddenly all of little Phasti's constant haranguing began making perfect sense. Hasti crept up towards the edge of the lake. She had worked out her strategy. The stag was standing foolishly at the end of a spit of mud, looking about and lowering his head for a drink every now and then. The breeze was blowing directly from him to her. But behind him, in the grass, she could see Masti, using the cover of the crooked tree to approach her target. She, too, was downwind of her target but she was directly upwind of Hasti's stag. The moment he smelt her he would bolt and Hasti had anticipated in which direction he would take off. Belly to the ground, she wriggled her way out onto an adjoining spit of mud and ducked behind the feathery reeds, watching and waiting.

The young stag was either supremely stupid or nasally challenged. Perhaps he never smelt Masti at all (even Hasti could smell her now) or didn't link her smell to danger. At any rate he only bolted when Masti sprang and brought down her kill. He turned and fled, straight towards Hasti, crouched in the reeds. The young tigress sprang and the stag stood no chance. He floundered in the water and went down.

Some distance away, Zafraan watched his sisters bring down the kills.

'Dear God, they've both scored hits. We're never going to hear the end of this!'

Little Phasti was dancing around in excitement. 'You did it, you did it, you did it, I love you, I love you, I love you!'

'Well done, girls!' Shaan-Bahadur licked his two thrilled elder daughters. 'That was poetry in motion!'

'And the dhimchack chick, sorry the girl with the silky tresses, photographed it all,' Naradmunni sang gleefully. 'You're all going to be famous again!'

Back at the village, Khoon-Pyaasa had taken his chance. He'd seen the tigers leave and then Ayesha follow. The village was empty. From the opposite side he entered and soon climbed up onto the roof of the headman's house. He lay flat half concealed by a chimney, looking directly down into the courtyard. Right in front of him, across the street was the temple with its little balcony where the girl usually set up her camera. He would hardly have to move to shoot both the tigers and girl. It was the perfect spot for an assassin... All he had to do was to wait.

It was a long wait, for out in the meadow, Shaan-Bahadur and his family feasted long and heavily on the double-kill. They could now relax for several days. Hasti and Masti of course, couldn't stop glowing. They finished most of the kill and dragged the remains under the cover of trees after Naradmunni had had his fill. From the sky, the Diclo-Fenac squadron planed down and were driven away by the infuriated tigers when they landed. Dum-kutta and the Gigglers too had caught wind of the kill, but had kept their distance, knowing how dangerous these fierce little tigers could be. It didn't really matter, in a matter of hours or so they would be dining on the fierce little tigers themselves...

The moon had risen, butter gold and large as a sovereign by the time the tiger family returned to the village. Her face glowing, Ayesha followed at a discreet distance and made her way up to the temple balcony. The full moon would provide enough light for some really unique night-time shots. Stiff and chilled, Khoon-Pyaasa waited and dozed on the rooftop. Then at last awoke… clutching his gun.

A terrible smile lit up his face. The courtyard below was bathed in silver moonlight. The great tiger was lying in the courtyard like some giant guard dog. The cubs were probably in the rooms. The jackal was curled up in the main doorway. And just across the street, he could see the moonlight glint off the big telephoto lenses of the photographer as she too kept vigil.

Khoon-Pyaasa swallowed and tightened his grip on his gun.

The tiger would be the first…

14

In an improvised burrow at the base of the tall cliffs, Col. 'Cuddles' Khujlimal briefed his band of suicide stabbers. Including his brother, Lieutenant Col. Kabab-me-Haddi, there were five crack fighters who would participate in the savage revenge attack.

'Right, so this is Operation Impale,' Col. Khujlimal said, rattling his quills for attention. 'Myself and Lieutenant Col. Kabab-me-Haddi will conduct the most dangerous part of the operation and may well be martyred…!' He outlined his diabolical plan as the suicide squad's eyes widened and several hundred quills quivered eagerly.

'It should be easy. Guerrilla tactics! Hit and run! That's what we're good at and that's what we'll do. The enemy won't even know what hit them. Remember, before they actually attack, they size each other up yowling hideously. All their attention is focused on the foe. That's when we go in, full tilt, handbrake turn, reverse, stab and zoom! The fools won't be expecting it! And then, if they do not kill each other then and there, all we have to do is to wait till the impaled quills take their effect and all the famous the tigers of the great Sher-kila National Park turn into man-eaters and are exterminated. Victory to Al-Seekh Kabab!'

'Al-Seekh Kabab zindabad, zindabad!'

'Good, now go and get some rest! We reconvene at 2230 hours! Dismiss!'

The porcupines dispersed, some digging up roots and tubers for an energy-supplying snack, others resting and revelling in the glory that was to be.

Lieutenant Col. Kabab-me-Haddi trotted along one of the high ridge paths, thinking this was his great chance to prove his courage—and later make a bid on his brother's leadership. He had fled during the first attack—tactically retreated actually—which was the sensible thing to do because he had lived to fight another day. Suddenly he drew up and paused... That smell? His nose twitched. He trundled ahead cautiously, round a bend and saw the deep rocky overhang. Waves of that dangerous scent were emerging from it, so thick as to be almost visible. Steeling himself—and ready to flee—he peered into the entrance.

A blood-curdling snarl roiled out of the cave. There at the back of the cave, in the gloom, a tigress lay on her side, her massive head raised, watching him, her eyes blazing amber, her lips drawn back in a snarl. Three tiny balls of charcoal-striped orange fur whimpered and mewled and suckled hungrily. In a flash, Kabab-me-Haddi recognized the tiger's smell: it was the same one that his valorous brother had stabbed after the failed raid.

'One inch closer and I'll make you eat your own quills!' the tigress snarled. But she stayed where she was. And then, Kabab-me-Haddi saw why: there were porcupine quills still sticking out of her chest and paws.

'Hahaha, hello Ms Pincushion!' he smirked, but kept his distance. You did not trifle with a tigress with cubs even if she was full of porcupine quills.

'Get out of here, you infection! You're stinking the place out!' the tigress snarled.

'Just going, just going...' Kabab-me-Haddi smirked. 'I thought you'd like to know...'

And what he told the tigress made Razia flatten her ears and snarl so terrifyingly that Kabab-me-Haddi beat a hasty retreat. 'See you later, ma'am! We'll let you know how things went...and then...' he gloated. Then, he'd lead the team here, so they could finish her off as well as her cubs.

The hit squad assembled at 2230 hours at the base of the tall cliffs.

'Right, we're off, single file, smart trot. Maintain complete quill silence at all times. And God be with us all!'

They set off, a grim column of six deadly rodents,

their mean eyes crimson with fanatic rage. They stopped just outside the village. Col. Khujlimal addressed the squad.

'Right, we split up here! You select suitable ambush points and wait... The enemy should appear at the stroke of the midnight hour! Major Prickles, you're in charge!'

'Yes, boss!'

'Come on, Chuboo-Chuboo!'

'Yes, Cuddles!'

'And don't call me Cuddles!'

The two porcupines disappeared into the undergrowth, heading for the temple. They sneaked into the courtyard via the rear entrance and stopped at the base of a peepul tree and began digging. This was what they were made for...

Lolita knew that something dangerous was in the air. Ever since she had opted out of the plan to exterminate Shaan-Bahadur and his family, she had been restless. Now she prowled the cliff ledges. She glanced at the blinding silver moon riding high. At around 2330 hours, she passed by the overhang where Razia lay, and sniffed, grimacing.

So! She had found the missing tigress and judging by the scents, warm, milky and nuzzly, it seemed that Razia had had her cubs. Better to stay away.

A low growl emanated from the cave.

'Lolita...'

'Sorry to disturb you, ma'am. Congratulations on your new family. I'm just leaving!'

'Wait!'

Lolita pricked up her ears. There had been pain in Razia's growl.

'You okay?'

'Come here...'

'Are you sure?'

'Come here!'

'Yes, ma'am!

A few minutes later, Lolita bounded out of the cave and raced down the ledges to the base of the cliff at a dangerous speed, pausing only to spray the big rocks en route with her startling news. She was a tigress with a mission! If only it was not too late.

A little earlier, Thug, Caligua and Taimur had met briefly, if uncomfortably, at the base of the cliffs and then set off through the grassy meadows towards the village. Resham, in her usual unpredictable way, had also decided to drop out of the raid: she, too, was confused. Rana Shaan-Bahadur had done something that went against all the tenets of honourable tiger behaviour and needed to be punished, but he was a damned handsome and courageous tiger too. Besides, there was something else she couldn't put her paw on... She wandered off amidst the rocks muttering under her breath.

The three males entered the main street of the village at 2350 hours. Five minutes later, curled up at the entrance of the headman's house, Naradmunni got the shock of his life when he opened his eyes. Thug was walking down the dusty track towards him followed by two other tigers—his henchmen. The tiger made no attempt to conceal himself.

'You, offal there, go call your boss!' he growled at poor Naradmunni.

Thug and his henchmen had been so focused on their mission they had failed to watch their backs. Keeping to the ditch that ran along one side of the path, the four ASKAA suicide stabbers followed the tigers.

'Huzoor, huzooor!' poor Naradmunni yelped, wondering why he was always the purveyor of bad news.

'What now? Shh…keep it down, the cubs are sleeping!'

'Huzoor, Shri Thugoutsideistalkswantstoyou…I mean Shri Thug is outside and wants to talk to you!'

'What does that fleabag want now?' Shaan-Bahadur rose languidly to his feet. 'Naradmunni, you watch over the cubs.'

'There are two others—Caligua and Taimur.'

'Oh, so the three stooges again, eh? No matter!'

Regally, Shaan-Bahadur emerged from the gateway and looked contemptuously down the street. Thug, flanked by Caligua and Taimur, was standing some way down, their tails flicking lazily.

'We're here to rip you and your family to shreds,' Thug said pleasantly. 'You're raising a family. No male tiger does that! Matter of honour! You have disgraced the species.'

'Dishonoured us! We spit upon you!'

'So we'll appreciate it if you cooperate!'

'An honour killing, you understand?'

'Any time, boys!' Shaan-Bahadur growled so malevolently that instinctively the three tigers took a step back. He flattened his ears and bared his teeth in a terrible rictus. His claws slipped out.

Thug swallowed and nodded. 'Okay boys, on the count of three... Taimur take the left flank, Caligua the right, I'll take him head on...'

Shaan-Bahadur knew the outcome would be bleak for him. Even if he managed to drive away the three, which was doubtful, he would in all likelihood be seriously injured in such a fight. He hoped the cubs would be able to take care of themselves and would have the sense to flee while he battled these louts.

'Naradmunni, I'm going to take on these fellows. Take the cubs and run for it!'

Poor Naradmunni nearly wept as he nodded and fled into the courtyard.

'Right...one...two...'

Shaan-Bahadur braced himself as he stared down his enemies. Then his green eyes widened.

'Look behind you, Thug,' he said nonchalantly.

'Hah! Don't try that one on me!'

'Thug, Thug, stop! Don't attack! It's a trap! It's a trap!'

Thug and his henchmen whirled around. Panting and heaving, with foam flecking her mouth, Lolita stood in the street trying to catch her breath. 'It's ASKAA! They've stabbed Razia, poor thing has had her cubs but is immobile. They're going to ambush you when you attack Shaan-Bahadur!'

'What? Stabbed Razia?'

Lolita gulped, almost overcome with emotion. 'Razia says she won't be able to hunt for some time, so you'll have to do that in order to feed her and the cubs!' She rolled her eyes eloquently. 'Don't you see? You can't kill Shaan-Bahadur now!'

'What the…? Thug's brain was scrambled.

'You can't kill Shaan-Bahadur!' Lolita screamed, 'Because now you're going to have to look after your own cubs until Razia gets well! Don't you get it?'

'Boss,' said Caligua laconically, 'are you going to listen to that airhead? Everyone knows what she has going with Shaan-Bahadur. She's just trying to protect him!'

'Yeah, she's a real fluffhead!' Taimur said, privately thinking that Lolita was really quite pretty.

'With a name like that, what can you expect?'

Thug nodded. 'Nice try, Lolita,' he said. 'It ain't going to work!'

He and the others turned their attention back to Shaan-Bahadur again.

'Wait! Wait! What she's said is true! Razia is full of porcupine quills and has helpless little cubs!'

Again, the three tigers whirled around.

Some distance behind Lolita, Resham stood, panting.

'Lolly left messages on the rocks everywhere and I went and checked on Razia myself! You can't attack Shaan-Bahadur now. No way!' she gulped. The moment she had seen Razia she had realized what had been bothering her: what if she had been in Raat-ki-Rani and now Razia's place and had had cubs? Who would have taken care of them? What had happened to poor Raat-ki-Rani and now Razia could happen to any tigress in the park.

Shaan-Bahadur glanced at Thug laconically. 'Welcome to the club, Thug,' he said.

In the ditch, the ASKAA hit team, which was about to scramble was also getting confused.

'They're supposed to attack him. Not have a tête-à-tête!'

'Boss, what should we do?'

'Didn't you hear that stupid tigress? Our cover is blown!' Major Prickles barked. 'We attack! Hit and run! Go, go, go!'

'Watch it fellows! Porcupine!' Shaan-Bahadur roared at the top of his voice, sending cracks down the walls of

village houses and setting off all the peacocks. For a long moment, Major Prickles stood stock still, staring at his enemy, his little eyes terror-struck, his eardrums almost ruptured by that rumble of deafening thunder. With a single bound Shaan-Bahadur was on to him and with a deft flick of his paw tossed the stunned Major high in the air. The Major somersaulted and landed upside down on two of the hit squad, causing a brief frenzy of fighting. Thug, Caligua and Taimur just stood, transfixed.

'The cubs!' Shaan-Bahadur growled, turning towards the doorway. The fourth member of the ASKAA suicide squad charged towards him. He did a very stylish handbrake turn and was about to cannon backwards into Shaan-Bahadur, whose back was now turned towards him, when he was whacked solidly across the face by a furious Lolita.

'Oh no, you don't... oww!' she yowled, smacking the porcupine senseless but getting four nasty quills embedded in her forepaw.

Inside the headman's compound, events had unfolded at a rapid pace.

At 2355 hours, Col. Khujlimal and Lieutenant Col. Kabab-me-Haddi broke through the floor in the right and left wings of the headman's house. The courtyard was empty and they could hear Shaan-Bahadur conversing with the other tigers in the street. The attack would happen at any time. Grimly they approached the front veranda, where they could see the cubs stretched out on the charpoys.

'This is going to be a cakewalk!' Col. Khujlimal muttered. 'We take two apiece!' He grinned, displaying his awful yellow buck teeth. 'Babies babies, wakey-wakey!' he called.

'Cuddles, there's someone on the roof!' Kabab-me-Haddi hissed.

Indeed there was, and sprawled there in his assassin's haven, Khoon-Pyaasa's brain too was scrambled. There were, what—one, two...three, four...no five tigers milling about in the street outside. Which one ought he to shoot? He squinted down the barrel of his gun, shifting his aim from one to the other, utterly confused. This was an embarrassment of riches!

And then came that roar that shook the walls and set the temple bell pinging and peacocks into hysterics. It was the roar of the devil welcoming you to his domain. Khoon-Pyaasa went white and passed out for a second. His gun slipped out of his grasp and slid down the roof falling harmlessly into the drain below. Desperately, he grabbed at it but found himself sliding backwards. Panic-stricken, he clutched at the tiles for grip. There was a crack as they gave way, now there was a hole in the roof, followed by more cracking...

A minute earlier, Col. Khujlimal had flicked a glance at the roof. 'Don't worry,' he barked, 'that fellow is also after the tigers. Come on, we carry out our mission now!'

They entered the veranda where the cubs had slipped down from the charpoys and were now watching them with wide if sleepy eyes.

'Babies!' hissed Col. Khujlimal sibilantly, 'come to Papa, hahaha!'

He pirouetted and his brother did the same, preparing to charge.

Phasti's green eyes glittered with excitement. 'Right, kids!' she yelled. 'Remember, vertical leap and swivel over them as they as they come, face them and take them out—we can do this, babies!'

That alas was doubtful. Hasti and Masti had eaten so much they could hardly move, let alone leap and swivel in midair as their little sister ordered. And Zafraan was just too laidback to try stunts like that.

Then they heard their father's great roar.

'That's Papa!' Masti said in relief.

'He's showing them!'

'And we'll show you babies!' Col. Khujlimal whispered evilly, squinting over his shoulder at Phasti to get his aim right.

Just then, a tile crashed down from the roof, smashing just beside him, followed by another... Col. Khujlimal felt a heavy but soft dead weight thump down on his back, squashing him flat, driving his own quills into his body and the air out of it from both ends. And then blackness rushed in.

'YOWWWW!' A blood-curdling scream rent the air as Khoon-Pyaasa scrambled to his feet, a veritable pincushion of quills—indeed a whole porcupine of quills, with the porcupine still attached sticking out of his bottom. Howling, he fled.

'Hey you, wait a minute, come back here! That's my brother you've got sticking out of your backside!' Lieutenant Col. Kabab-me-Haddi couldn't believe his eyes. Furious, he lined up Hasti and Masti and engaged reverse.

'Sorry, I can't let you do that!' Zafraan said lazily, bringing down a hefty paw on the porcupine's forehead as it shot past him. (He'd had a lot of practice swatting bluebottles.)

'Well done, bro!' Phasti's eyes shone; she was thrilled. Imagine! All three of her protégés had surpassed themselves in a single day! Lieutenant Col. Kabab-me-Haddi reeled around, drunkenly shedding quills and then fled, screaming blue murder.

Outside, Rana Shaan-Bahadur glanced at Lolita who was limping about, but looking beatific. 'Thank you,' he said. 'I'll check on the cubs and then pull those out for you!'

Lolita staggered around on three paws, dazed with happiness.

Shaan-Bahadur backed away from the doorway as a human being with a porcupine attached to his rear suddenly erupted out of the compound screaming, followed by another hysterical porcupine.

'Human beings and that ASKAA lot,' he remarked, 'they're both completely mental.' He bounded inside.

'Kids!'

'They're safe, huzoor, the cubs are safe!' Naradmunni suddenly appeared by his side. No one knew where he had disappeared during the fracas.

'Papa, we're good!'

'We sent them packing.'

'Such lily-livered cowards, those porcupines! You can whack 'em like swatting flies!' That of course was Zafraan.

'Oh God,' Hasti moaned, 'now we're never going to hear the end of it.'

'Did you see my technique? Absolutely brilliant! Superb anticipation, perfect timing and whack! Speed, economy, beauty!'

'Gettim girls!'

'Gotta go now, catch up with you later!' Thug muttered to Shaan-Bahadur a little later, looking sheepish. Caligua and Taimur paced about restlessly in the background, still trying to figure out exactly what had happened. Shaan-Bahadur grinned.

'The begum and babies beckon, eh?'

Thug grinned back. 'Looks like your kids are calling you again, too!'

In the doorway, four young faces looked out eagerly at Shaan-Bahadur.

'Papa, let's go and hunt porcupines!'

'I think we've had enough of porcupines for one night!'

Thug paused. 'Um…there's one more thing…' He looked irritably at Caligua and Taimur who had stopped pacing and were all ears. 'Haven't you two got anything better to do?' he snapped. The tigers withdrew. Thug cleared his throat.

'Um… I'm sorry for all…all the trouble we caused you and your family…' he muttered. 'Never realized… it was unforgivable.'

Shaan-Bahadur nodded. 'It's okay, times change. I learnt that too… Some traditions are plain stupid.'

'It would have been most dishonourable…'

'Forget it, Thug.'

'Yes, boss!'

Crouched down in the temple veranda, Ayesha of the silken tresses kept her eyes glued to her viewfinder as the astonishing events unfolded before her that night. At last she switched off her tired cameras, hardly believing what she had seen and filmed on this brilliantly moonlit night. She didn't know it then but her film would win her eight awards at the following year's Oscars.

There is not much to add.

Khoon-Pyaasa, with Col. 'Cuddles' Khujlimal still attached to his rear, just disappeared and was never seen again.

Lieutenant Col. Kabab-me-Haddi went berserk and after stabbing several members of the Gigglers who had been hanging around near the village, backed into a tree so hard, he jammed his quick release mechanism and got stuck there, until the cubs found him the next day…

The other members of ASKAA disappeared underground.

Dum-kutta is still hoping his tail will re-grow and has been consuming all sorts of weird herbs and gross animal parts towards that end.

The Diclo-Fenacs, alas, only heard of what had happened the following morning. Tragically, there were no dead bodies strewn around in Taboo Valley as they had hoped.

Rana Shaan-Bahadur retained his title as alpha male of Sher-kila National Park. He and his cubs are now getting a bit tired of being treated like celebrity film stars, but there's nothing they can do about it except growl and bear it.

Thug has his paws full dealing with his three rambunctious cubs and readily relinquished the position he had usurped from Shaan-Bahadur.

Razia recovered completely, but pretended she hadn't for several months after she actually had, so that Thug could properly bond with the cubs and she could chill. Both she and Resham privately admitted that Rana Shaan-Bahadur had done a pretty good job as a daddy to his cubs.

The cubs, Hasti, Masti, Phasti and the lordly Zafraan, would remain with their father (and hunt porcupines) for around two years before setting off to make lives for themselves.

As for the lovely Lolita, well, she's First Tigress now and soon thereafter disappeared into a cave whose location is unknown...

'Congratulations, huzoor! Three beautiful babies!' Naradmunni came rushing up to Shaan-Bahadur one morning, shortly afterwards. 'Two boys and a girl this time!' He smiled. 'And that dhimchak chick photographer from the *National Geographic*—she's back. She wants to make *The Tigers of Taboo Valley 2*.

'Oh God,' groaned Rana Shaan-Bahadur shaking his shaggy head, 'it's starting all over again!'